MW00614651

HYMNS AND CHORUSES
WITH GUITAR CHORDS

HOW SWEET
THE SOUND

ABINGDON PRESS
Nashville

How Sweet the Sound:
Hymns and Choruses with Guitar Chords

This book is printed on acid-free, recycled paper.

ISBN 978-0-687-08995-6

09 10 11 12 13 – 10 9 8 7 6 5

MANUFACTURED IN THE UNITED STATES OF AMERICA

O For a Thousand Tongues to Sing

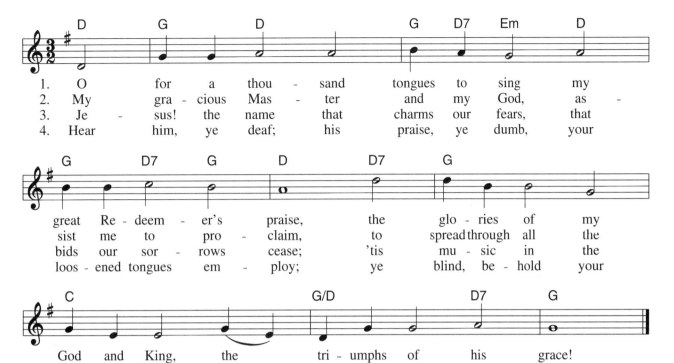

1. O for a thou - sand tongues to sing my
2. My gra - cious Mas - ter and my God, as -
3. Je - sus! the name that charms our fears, that
4. Hear him, ye deaf; his praise, ye dumb, your

great Re - deem - er's praise, the glo - ries of my
sist me to pro - claim, to spread through all the
bids our sor - rows cease; 'tis mu - sic in the
loos - ened tongues em - ploy; ye blind, be - hold your

God and King, the tri - umphs of his grace!
earth a - broad the hon - ors of thy name.
sin - ner's ears, 'tis life and health, and peace.
Sav - ior come, and leap, ye lame, for joy.

WORDS: Charles Wesley
MUSIC: Carl G. Gläser

Blessed Be the Name

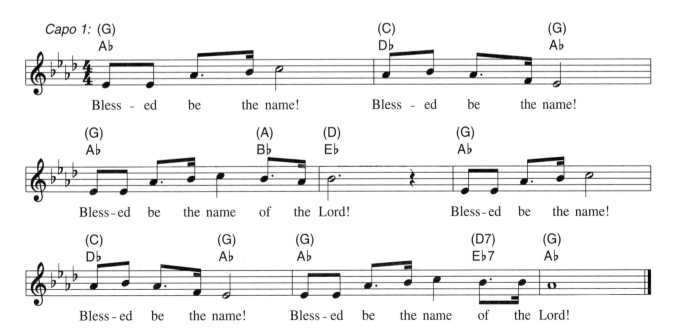

Bless - ed be the name! Bless - ed be the name!

Bless - ed be the name of the Lord! Bless - ed be the name!

Bless - ed be the name! Bless - ed be the name of the Lord!

WORDS: USA campmeeting chorus
MUSIC: USA campmeeting melody

3

Holy, Holy, Holy

1. Ho - ly, ho - ly, ho - ly! Lord God Al - might - y!
2. Ho - ly, ho - ly, ho - ly! All the saints a - dore thee,
3. Ho - ly, ho - ly, ho - ly! Though the dark - ness hide thee,
4. Ho - ly, ho - ly, ho - ly! Lord God Al - might - y!

Ear - ly in the morn - ing our song shall rise to thee.
cast - ing down their gold - en crowns a - round the glass - y sea;
though the eye of sin - ful man thy glo - ry may not see,
All thy works shall praise thy name, in earth and sky and sea.

Ho - ly, ho - ly, ho - ly! Mer - ci - ful and might - y,
cher - u - bim and ser - a - phim fall - ing down be - fore thee,
on - ly thou art ho - ly; there is none be - side thee,
Ho - ly, ho - ly, ho - ly! Mer - ci - ful and might - y,

God in three per - sons, bless - ed Trin - i - ty!
which wert, and art, and ev - er - more shall be.
per - fect in power, in love and pur - i - ty.
God in three per - sons, bless - ed Trin - i - ty!

WORDS: Reginald Heber
MUSIC: John B. Dykes

4

Glory Be to the Father

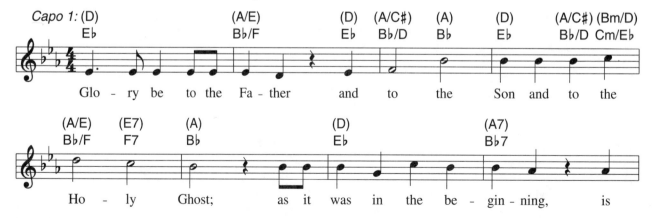

Glo - ry be to the Fa - ther and to the Son and to the

Ho - ly Ghost; as it was in the be - gin - ning, is

WORDS: Lesser Doxology
MUSIC: Henry W. Greatorex

now, and ev - er shall be, world with-out end. A - men. A - men.

We, Thy People, Praise Thee

We, thy peo - ple, praise thee, praise thee, God of ev - ery

na - tion! We, thy peo - ple, praise thee, praise thee,

Lord of Hosts e - ter - nal!
1. Days of won - der, days of beau - ty,
2. For thy bless - ings, for thy boun - ty,

days of rap - ture filled with light tell thy good - ness,
joy - ful songs to thee we sing, songs of glo - ry,

tell thy mer - cies, tell thy glo - rious might. We, thy peo - ple,
songs of tri - umph to our God and King.

praise thee, praise thee, praise thee ev - er - more!

WORDS: Kate Stearns Page
MUSIC: Franz Joseph Haydn

6 **Come, Thou Almighty King**

1. Come, thou al - might - y King, help us thy
2. Come, thou in - car - nate Word, gird on thy
3. Come, ho - ly Com - fort - er, thy sa - cred
4. To thee, great One in Three, e - ter - nal

name to sing, help us to praise! Fa - ther all -
might - y sword, our prayer at - tend! Come, and thy
wit - ness bear in this glad hour. Thou who al -
prais - es be, hence, ev - er - more. Thy sov - ereign

glo - ri - ous, o'er all vic - to - ri - ous,
peo - ple bless, and give thy word suc - cess;
might - y art, now rule in ev - ery heart,
maj - es - ty may we in glo - ry see,

come and reign o - ver us, An - cient of Days!
Spir - it of ho - li - ness, on us de - scend!
and ne'er from us de - part, Spir - it of power!
and to e - ter - ni - ty love and a - dore!

WORDS: Anonymous
MUSIC: Felice de Giardini

7 **Glory Be to the Father**

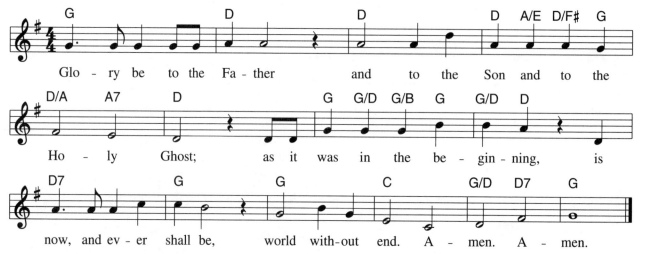

Glo - ry be to the Fa - ther and to the Son and to the

Ho - ly Ghost; as it was in the be - gin - ning, is

now, and ev - er shall be, world with-out end. A - men. A - men.

WORDS: Lesser Doxology
MUSIC: Charles Meineke

O Worship the King

1. O worship the King, all glorious above, O grateful ly sing God's power and God's love; our Shield and Defend er, the Ancient of Days, pavilioned in splendor, and girded with praise.

2. O tell of God's might, O sing of God's grace, whose robe is the light, whose canopy space, whose chariots of wrath the deep thunder clouds form, and dark is God's path on the wings of the storm.

3. Thy bountiful care, what tongue can recite? It breathes in the air, it shines in the light; it streams from the hills, it descends to the plain, and sweetly distills in the dew and the rain.

4. Frail children of dust, and feeble as frail, in thee do we trust, nor find thee to fail; thy mercies how tender, how firm to the end, our Maker, Defender, Redeemer, and Friend.

WORDS: Robert Grant
MUSIC: Attr. to Johann Michael Haydn

Praise God, from Whom All Blessings Flow

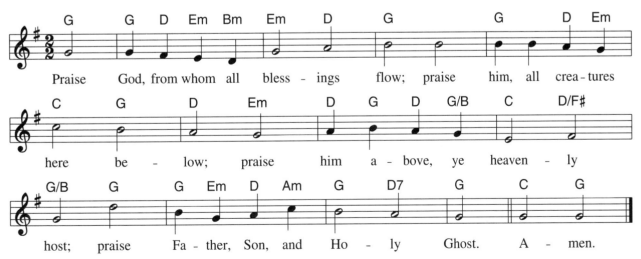

Praise God, from whom all blessings flow; praise him, all creatures here below; praise him above, ye heavenly host; praise Father, Son, and Holy Ghost. A-men.

WORDS: Thomas Ken
MUSIC: Attr. to Louis Bourgeois

10 How Great Thou Art

WORDS and MUSIC: Stuart K. Hine

¡Canta, Débora, Canta!

¡Can - ta, Dé - bo - ra, can - ta! ¡Can - ta, Dé - bo - ra, can - ta!

Ma - dre de Is - ra - el, li - der de e - jér - ci - tos, can - ta un him - no a tu Se -
Moth - er of Is - ra - el, lead - er of her ar - mies, sing a hymn of vic - tory to our

Estribillo (Refrain)

ñor. Por - que bue - no es Dios, bue - no es Dios, él es -
God. For our God is good! God is good, and has

co - ge a los hu - mil - des. Por - que bue - no es Dios,
cho - sen those who are hum - ble. For our God is good!

bue - no es Dios, él los for - ta - le - ce con su po - der.
God is good, and will strength - en the peo - ple with might!

WORDS and MUSIC: Luiza Cruz; English trans. Gertrude C. Suppe; Spanish trans. Raquel Gutiérrez-Achon
© 1975, 1987 The United Methodist Publishing House; trans. © 1989 The United Methodist Publishing House

Heleluyan
(Alleluia)

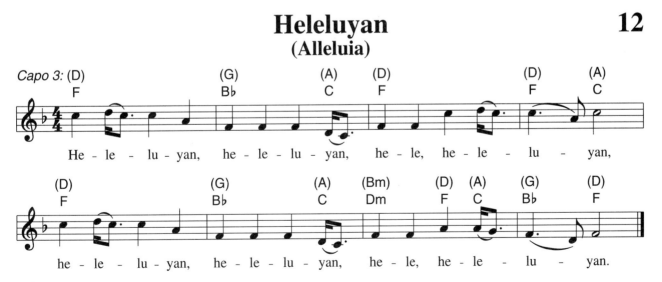

Capo 3: (D)   (G)   (A) (D)   (D) (A)
F   B♭   C F   F C

He - le - lu - yan, he - le - lu - yan, he - le, he - le - lu - yan,

(D)   (G)   (A) (Bm) (D) (A) (G) (D)
F   B♭   C Dm   F C B♭ F

he - le - lu - yan, he - le - lu - yan, he - le, he - le - lu - yan.

WORDS: Trad. Muscogee (Creek) Indian
MUSIC: Trad. Muscogee (Creek) Indian; trans. Charles H. Webb
Trans. © 1989 The United Methodist Publishing House

13 Joyful, Joyful, We Adore Thee

1. Joy - ful, joy - ful, we a - dore thee, God of glo - ry,
2. All thy works with joy sur - round thee, earth and heaven re -
3. Thou art giv - ing and for - giv - ing, ev - er bless - ing,
4. Mor - tals, join the might - y cho - rus which the morn - ing

Lord of love; hearts un - fold like flowers be - fore thee,
flect thy rays, stars and an - gels sing a - round thee,
ev - er blest, well - spring of the joy of liv - ing,
stars be - gan; love di - vine is reign - ing o'er us,

open - ing to the sun a - bove. Melt the clouds of
cen - ter of un - bro - ken praise. Field and for - est,
o - cean depth of hap - py rest! Thou our Fa - ther,
bind - ing all with - in its span. Ev - er sing - ing,

sin and sad - ness; drive the dark of
vale and moun - tain, flow - ery mead - ow,
Christ our broth - er, all who live in
march we on - ward, vic - tors in the

doubt a - way. Giv - er of im -
flash - ing sea, chant - ing bird and
love are thine; teach us how to
midst of strife; joy - ful mu - sic

mor - tal glad - ness, fill us with the light of day!
flow - ing foun - tain, call us to re - joice in thee.
love each oth - er, lift us to the joy di - vine.
leads us sun - ward, in the tri - umph song of life.

WORDS: Henry Van Dyke; st. 4 alt.
MUSIC: Ludwig van Beethoven

To God Be the Glory

WORDS: Fanny J. Crosby
MUSIC: William H. Doane

15

My Tribute

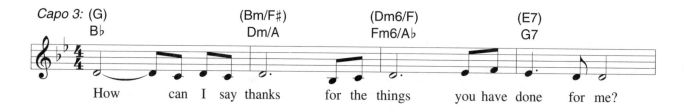

How can I say thanks for the things you have done for me?

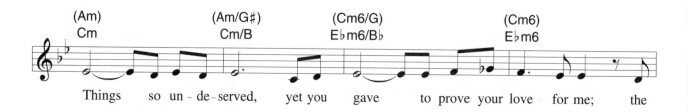

Things so un-de-served, yet you gave to prove your love for me; the

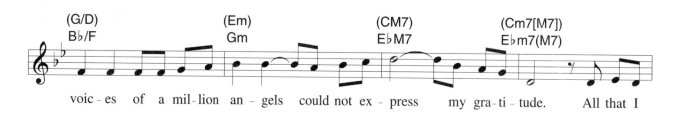

voic-es of a mil-lion an-gels could not ex-press my gra-ti-tude. All that I

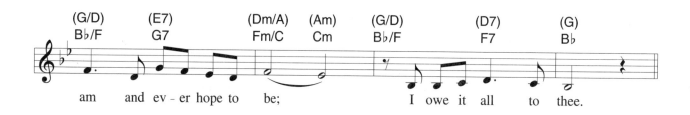

am and ev-er hope to be; I owe it all to thee.

Refrain

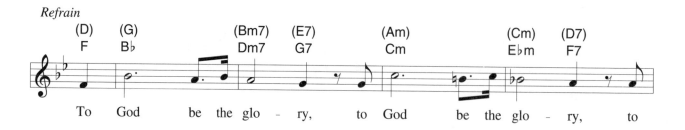

To God be the glo-ry, to God be the glo-ry, to

God be the glo-ry for the things he has done. With his

WORDS and MUSIC: Andraé Crouch

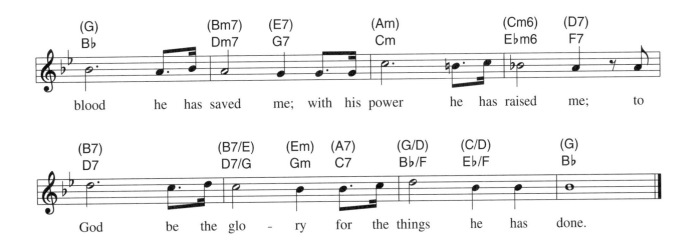

blood   he has saved   me;   with   his power   he has raised   me;   to

God   be   the glo - ry   for   the things   he   has   done.

For the Beauty of the Earth

1. For   the   beau - ty   of   the   earth,   for   the   glo - ry
2. For   the   beau - ty   of   each   hour   of   the   day   and
3. For   the   joy   of   hu - man   love,   broth - er,   sis - ter,
4. For   thy - self,   best   Gift   Di - vine,   to   the   world   so

of   the   skies,   for   the   love   which   from   our   birth
of   the   night,   hill   and   vale,   and   tree   and   flower,
par - ent,   child,   friends   on   earth   and   friends   a - bove,
free - ly   given,   for   that   great,   great   love   of   thine,

Refrain

o - ver   and   a - round   us   lies;
sun   and   moon,   and   stars   of   light;   } Lord   of   all,   to
for   all   gen - tle   thoughts   and   mild;
peace   on   earth,   and   joy   in   heaven;

thee   we   raise   this   our   hymn   of   grate - ful   praise.

WORDS: Folliot S. Pierpoint
MUSIC: Conrad Kocher; arr. W. H. Monk

17   I Love You, Lord

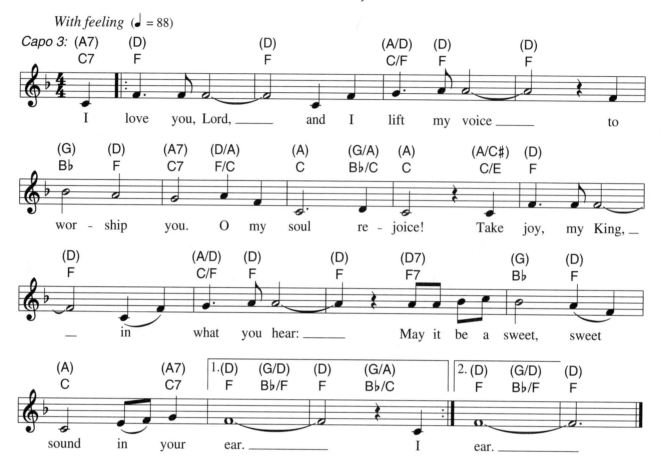

With feeling (♩ = 88)

Capo 3:

I love you, Lord, _____ and I lift my voice _____ to wor - ship you. O my soul re - joice! Take joy, my King, _ _ in what you hear: _____ May it be a sweet, sweet sound in your ear. _____ I ear. _____

WORDS and MUSIC: Laurie Klein

18   We Will Glorify

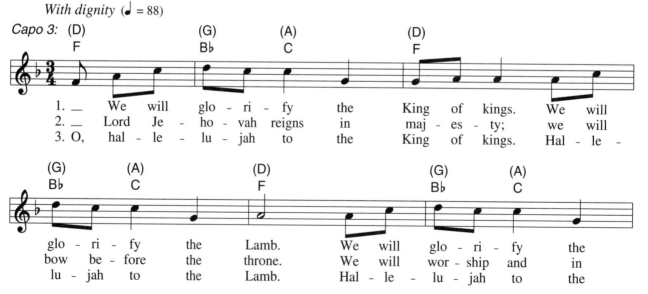

With dignity (♩ = 88)

Capo 3:

1. _ We will glo - ri - fy the King of kings. We will
2. _ Lord Je - ho - vah reigns in maj - es - ty; we will
3. O, hal - le - lu - jah to the King of kings. Hal - le -

glo - ri - fy the Lamb. We will glo - ri - fy the
bow be - fore the throne. We will wor - ship and in
lu - jah to the Lamb. Hal - le - lu - jah to the

WORDS and MUSIC: Twila Paris

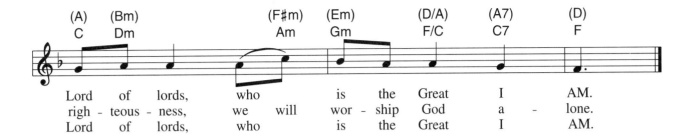

Lord of lords, who is the Great I AM.
righ - teous - ness, we will wor - ship God a - lone.
Lord of lords, who is the Great I AM.

How Majestic Is Your Name

19

With energy (♩ = 172)

O Lord our Lord, how ma - jes - tic is your name in all the

earth. O Lord our Lord, how ma - jes - tic is your name in all the

earth. O Lord _____ we praise your

name, O Lord _____ we mag - ni - fy your

name, Prince of Peace, might - y God. O Lord God Al -

might - y. O y. _____

WORDS and MUSIC: Michael W. Smith

20   # Clap Your Hands

Gentle Rock (♩ = 132)

Clap your hands! Clap your hands! Sing a new song in
cel - e - bra - tion! Clap your hands! Clap your hands!
Sing a new song in cel - e - bra - tion! Clap your hands!
Clap your hands! God is great! We praise our God with song!
God is great! We praise our God with song!

WORDS and MUSIC: Handt Hanson and Paul Murakami

21   # Glorify Your Name

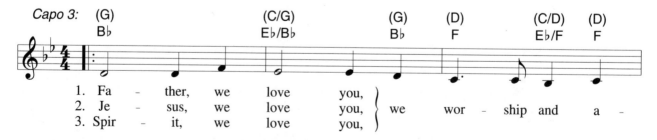

Capo 3:

1. Fa - ther, we love you,
2. Je - sus, we love you,
3. Spir - it, we love you,
we wor - ship and a -

WORDS and MUSIC: Donna Adkins

dore you, glo - ri - fy your name in all the earth. _____

Glo - ri - fy your name, glo - ri - fy your

name, glo - ri - fy your name in all the earth. _____

earth. _____

We Worship and Adore You

22

We wor - ship and a - dore you, bow - ing down be -

fore you, songs of prais - es sing - ing, hal - le - lu - jahs

ring - ing. Hal - le - lu - jah! Hal - le

lu - jah! Hal - le - lu - jah! A - men!

WORDS and MUSIC: Traditional

23

Lord, Be Glorified

Simply, expressively (♩ = 76)

In my life, Lord, be glo - ri - fied, be glo - ri - fied. In my life, Lord, be glo - ri - fied to - day.

2. In your church, Lord,
4. In our songs, Lord,
3. In our lives, Lord,
5. In our work, Lord,
6. In our worship,

WORDS and MUSIC: Bob Kilpatrick

24

O Lord, You're Beautiful

Meditatively (♩ = 52)

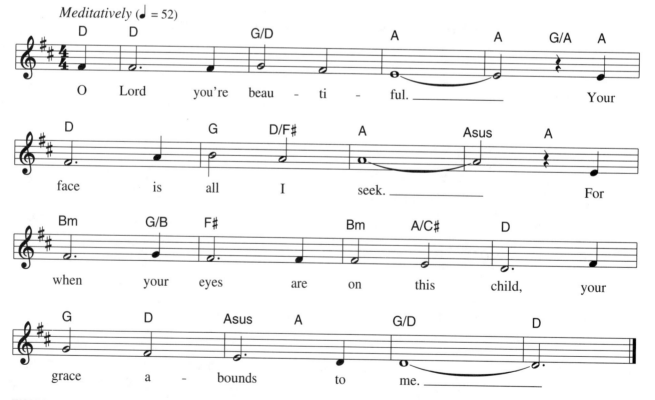

O Lord you're beau - ti - ful. _____ Your face is all I seek. _____ For when your eyes are on this child, your grace a - bounds to me. _____

WORDS: Psalm 34:15 and Keith Green
MUSIC: Keith Green

I Will Call upon the Lord

25

WORDS and MUSIC: Michael O'Shields

26 A Mighty Fortress Is Our God

WORDS: Martin Luther; trans. Frederick H. Hedge
MUSIC: Martin Luther

Your Love, O God

WORDS: Anders Frostenson; trans. Fred Kaan
MUSIC: Lars Åke Lundberg

Trans. © 1974 Hope Publishing Co.; music by permission of Lars Åke Lundberg

28

O God, Our Help in Ages Past

| | C | C | F | C/E | Am | Dm7 | G | C |

1. O God, our help in a - ges past, our
2. Be - fore the hills in or - der stood, or
3. A thou - sand a - ges, in thy sight, are
4. O God, our help in a - ges past, our

| Am | Em | Am/C | D | G | | C | F | Dm | G |

hope for years to come, our shel - ter from the
earth re - ceived her frame, from ev - er - last - ing,
like an eve - ning gone; short as the watch that
hope for years to come; be thou our guide while

| C | F | E | C/E | F | C | Dm/F | G | C |

storm - y blast, and our e - ter - nal home!
thou art God, to end - less years the same.
ends the night, be - fore the ris - ing sun.
life shall last, and our e - ter - nal home.

WORDS: Isaac Watts
MUSIC: Attr. to William Croft

29

God of the Sparrow God of the Whale

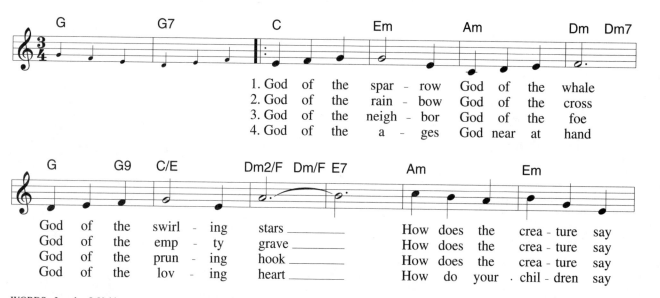

| G | G7 | C | Em | Am | Dm Dm7 |

1. God of the spar - row God of the whale
2. God of the rain - bow God of the cross
3. God of the neigh - bor God of the foe
4. God of the a - ges God near at hand

| G | G9 C/E | Dm2/F Dm/F E7 | Am | Em |

God of the swirl - ing stars _____ How does the crea - ture say
God of the emp - ty grave _____ How does the crea - ture say
God of the prun - ing hook _____ How does the crea - ture say
God of the lov - ing heart _____ How do your chil - dren say

WORDS: Jaroslav J. Vajda
MUSIC: Carl F. Schalk

Words © 1983 Jaroslav J. Vajda; music © 1983 G.I.A. Publications, Inc.

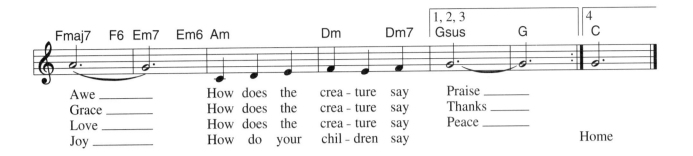

God Will Take Care of You

30

WORDS: Civilla D. Martin
MUSIC: W. Stillman Martin

31 He Leadeth Me: O Blessed Thought

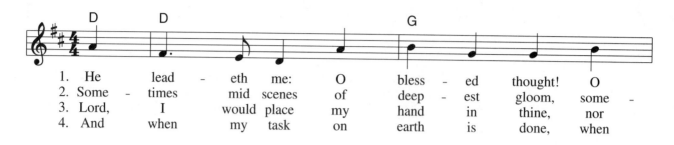

1. He lead - eth me: O bless - ed thought! O
2. Some - times mid scenes of deep - est gloom, some -
3. Lord, I would place my hand in thine, nor
4. And when my task on earth is done, when

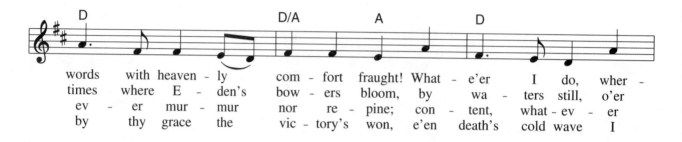

words with heaven - ly com - fort fraught! What - e'er I do, wher -
times where E - den's bow - ers bloom, by wa - ters still, o'er
ev - er mur - mur nor re - pine; con - tent, what - ev - er
by thy grace the vic - tory's won, e'en death's cold wave I

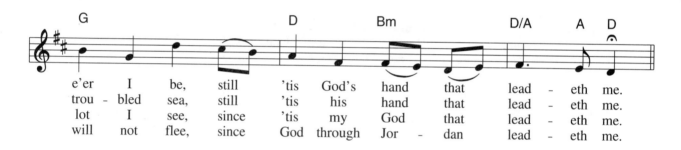

e'er I be, still 'tis God's hand that lead - eth me.
trou - bled sea, still 'tis his hand that lead - eth me.
lot I see, since 'tis my God that lead - eth me.
will not flee, since God through Jor - dan lead - eth me.

He lead - eth me, he lead - eth me, by

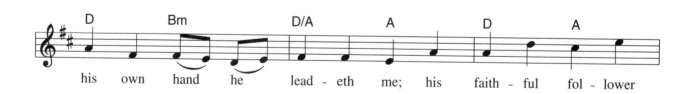

his own hand he lead - eth me; his faith - ful fol - lower

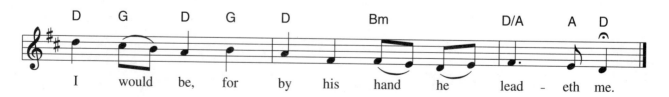

I would be, for by his hand he lead - eth me.

WORDS: Joseph H. Gilmore
MUSIC: William B. Bradbury

Great Is Thy Faithfulness

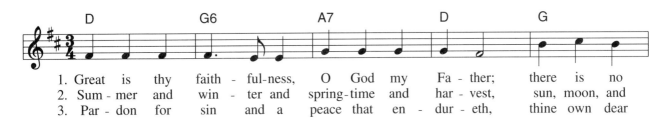

1. Great is thy faith - ful-ness, O God my Fa - ther; there is no
2. Sum - mer and win - ter and spring-time and har - vest, sun, moon, and
3. Par - don for sin and a peace that en - dur - eth, thine own dear

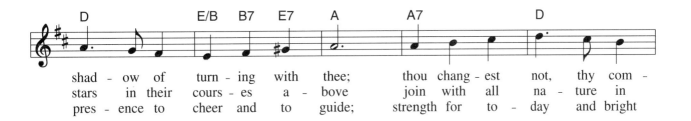

shad - ow of turn - ing with thee; thou chang - est not, thy com -
stars in their cours - es a - bove join with all na - ture in
pres - ence to cheer and to guide; strength for to - day and bright

pas - sions, they fail not; as thou hast been, thou for - ev - er wilt
man - i - fold wit - ness to thy great faith - ful - ness, mer - cy, and
hope for to - mor - row, bless - ings all mine, with ten thou - sand be -

Refrain

be.
love. } Great is thy faith - ful-ness! Great is thy faith - ful-ness!
side!

Morn - ing by morn - ing new mer - cies I see; all I have need - ed thy

hand hath pro - vid - ed; great is thy faith - ful - ness, Lord, un - to me!

WORDS: Thomas O. Chisholm
MUSIC: William M. Runyan

33   Children of the Heavenly Father

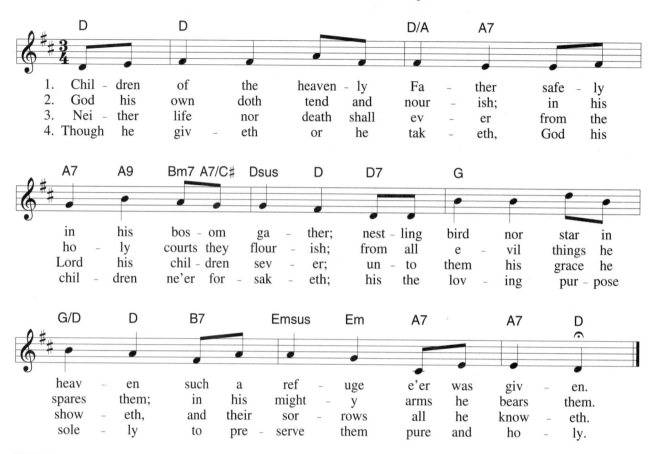

1. Chil - dren of the heaven - ly Fa - ther safe - ly
2. God his own doth tend and nour - ish; in his
3. Nei - ther life nor death shall ev - er from the
4. Though he giv - eth or he tak - eth, God his

in his bos - om ga - ther; nest - ling bird nor star in
ho - ly courts they flour - ish; from all e - vil things he
Lord his chil - dren sev - er; un - to them his grace he
chil - dren ne'er for - sak - eth; his the lov - ing pur - pose

heav - en such a ref - uge e'er was giv - en.
spares them; in his might - y arms he bears them.
show - eth, and their sor - rows all he know - eth.
sole - ly to pre - serve them pure and ho - ly.

WORDS: Caroline V. Sandell-Berg; trans. Ernst W. Olson
MUSIC: Swedish melody

34   Praise the Name of Jesus

Simply (♩ = 96)

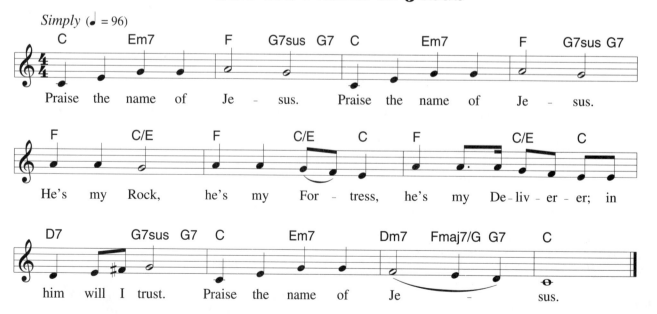

Praise the name of Je - sus. Praise the name of Je - sus.

He's my Rock, he's my For - tress, he's my De - liv - er - er; in

him will I trust. Praise the name of Je - sus.

WORDS and MUSIC: Roy Hicks, Jr.

Leaning on the Everlasting Arms

WORDS: Elisha A. Hoffman
MUSIC: Anthony J. Showalter

36 # On Eagle's Wings

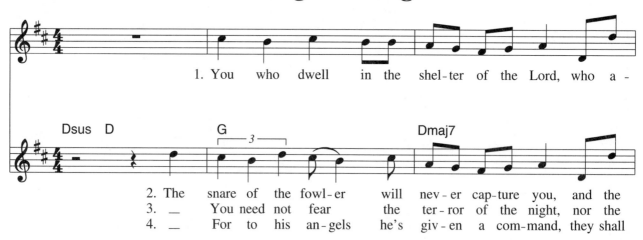

1. You who dwell in the shel-ter of the Lord, who a-

2. The snare of the fowl-er will nev-er cap-ture you, and the
3. __ You need not fear the ter-ror of the night, nor the
4. __ For to his an-gels he's giv-en a com-mand, they shall

bide in his sha-dow for life, __ say to the Lord: "My
fam-ine will bring you no fear, __ un-der his wings your
ar-row that flies by day, __ though thou-sands fall a-
guard you in all of your ways: up-on their hands they will

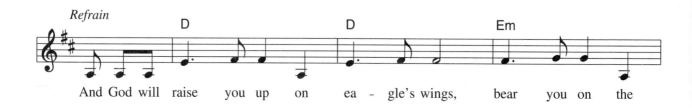

Cue notes for Stanza 4

ref - uge, my Rock in whom I trust!"
ref - uge, his faith - ful - ness your shield.
bout you, but near you it will not come.
bear you up, lest you dash your foor a - gainst a stone.

Refrain

And God will raise you up on ea - gle's wings, bear you on the

breath of dawn, make you to shine like the sun, and

WORDS and MUSIC: Michael Joncas

hold   you   in   the   palm   of   God's   hand.

We Gather Together

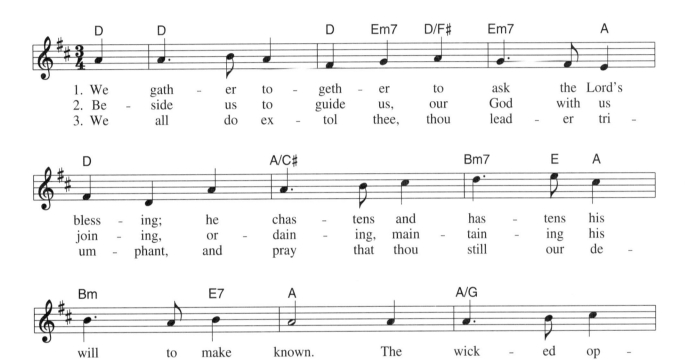

1. We   gath – er   to – geth – er   to   ask   the Lord's
2. Be – side   us   to   guide   us,   our   God   with   us
3. We   all   do ex – tol   thee,   thou   lead – er   tri –

bless – ing;   he   chas – tens   and   has – tens   his
join – ing,   or – dain – ing, main – tain – ing   his
um – phant,   and   pray   that   thou   still   our   de –

will   to   make   known.   The   wick – ed   op –
king – dom   di – vine;   so   from   the   be –
fend – er   wilt   be.   Let   thy   con – gre –

press – ing   now   cease   from   dis – tress – ing.   Sing
gin – ning   the   fight   we   were   win – ning;   thou,
ga – tion   es – cape   trib – u – la – tion;   thy

prais – es   to   his   name;   he   for – gets   not   his   own.
Lord,   wast   at   our   side,   all   glo – ry   be   thine!
name   be   ev – er   praised!   O   Lord,   make   us   free!

WORDS: *Nederlandtsch Gedenckclanck*; trans. Theodore Baker
MUSIC: 16th cent. Dutch melody

38 Awesome God

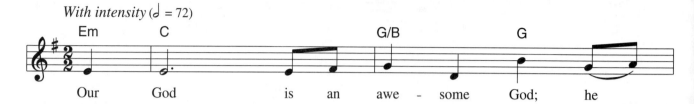

Our God is an awe-some God; he

reigns from heav-en a-bove with wis - dom,

power, and love. Our God is an awe-some God!

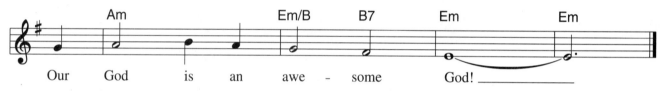

Our God is an awe - some God!

WORDS and MUSIC: Rich Mullins

Holy, Holy

WORDS and MUSIC: Jimmy Owens

40   O Mary, Don't You Weep

Refrain

O Mary, don't you weep, don't you mourn, O Mary, don't you

weep, don't you mourn; Pha - raoh's ar - my got drown - ded,

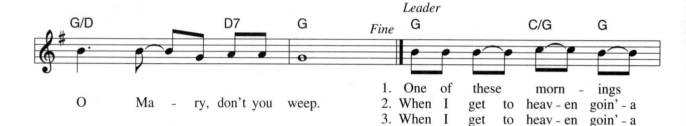

O Mary, don't you weep.

Leader

1. One of these morn - ings
2. When I get to heav - en goin' - a
3. When I get to heav - en goin' - a

bright and fair, goin' - a take my wings and cleave the air;
sing and shout, ain't no - bod - y there goin' - a turn me out;
put on my shoes, goin' - a run a - bout and spread the news;

All

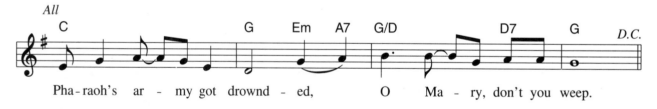

Pha - raoh's ar - my got drownd - ed, O Ma - ry, don't you weep.

WORDS and MUSIC: African American spiritual

41   Jesus, Name Above All Names

Gentle lilting (♩. = 66)

Je - sus Name a - bove all names, beau - ti - ful Sav - ior

WORDS and MUSIC: Naida Hearn

glo - ri - ous Lord. Em - man - u - el, God is

with us, bless-ed Re - deem - er, liv - ing Word.

Behold, What Manner of Love

42

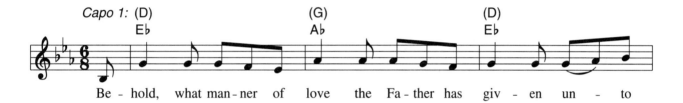

Be - hold, what man-ner of love the Fa - ther has giv - en un - to

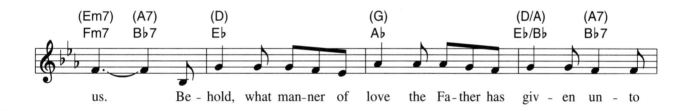

us. Be - hold, what man-ner of love the Fa - ther has giv - en un - to

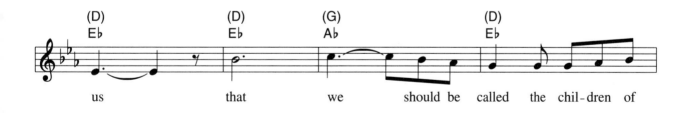

us that we should be called the chil-dren of

God, that we should be called the chil-dren of God.

WORDS and MUSIC: Pat Van Tine

43 He Is Exalted

WORDS and MUSIC: Twila Paris

Great Is the Lord

45

This Is My Father's World

WORDS: Maltbie D. Babcock
MUSIC: Trad. English melody; adapt. Franklin L. Sheppard

46

Morning Has Broken

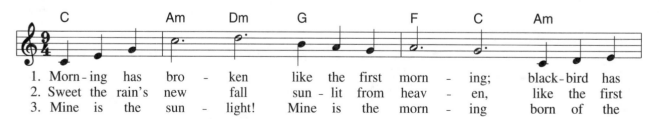

1. Morn - ing has bro - ken like the first morn - ing; black-bird has
2. Sweet the rain's new fall sun - lit from heav - en, like the first
3. Mine is the sun - light! Mine is the morn - ing born of the

WORDS: Eleanor Farjeon
MUSIC: Trad. Gaelic melody
Words by permission of David Higham Associates, Ltd.

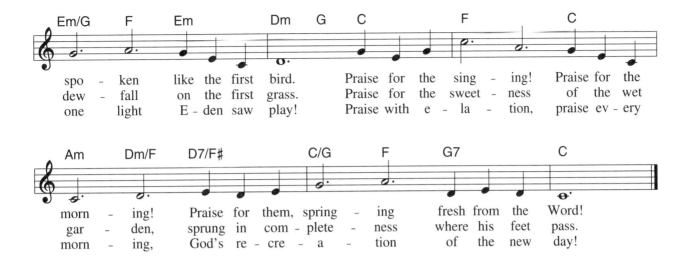

spo - ken like the first bird. Praise for the sing - ing! Praise for the
dew - fall on the first grass. Praise for the sweet - ness of the wet
one light E - den saw play! Praise with e - la - tion, praise ev - ery

morn - ing! Praise for them, spring - ing fresh from the Word!
gar - den, sprung in com - plete - ness where his feet pass.
morn - ing, God's re - cre - a - tion of the new day!

All Things Bright and Beautiful 47

Refrain

All things bright and beau - ti - ful, all crea - tures great and small,

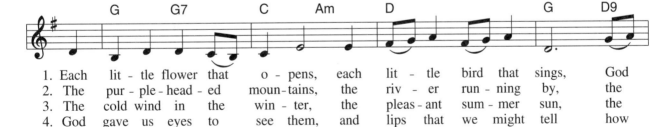

all things wise and won - der - ful: the Lord God made them all.

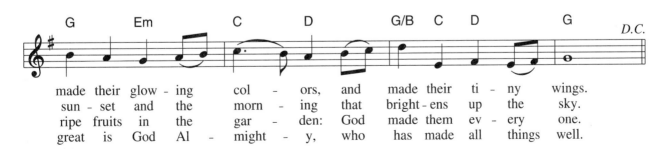

1. Each lit - tle flower that o - pens, each lit - tle bird that sings, God
2. The pur - ple - head - ed moun - tains, the riv - er run - ning by, the
3. The cold wind in the win - ter, the pleas - ant sum - mer sun, the
4. God gave us eyes to see them, and lips that we might tell how

made their glow - ing col - ors, and made their ti - ny wings.
sun - set and the morn - ing that bright - ens up the sky.
ripe fruits in the gar - den: God made them ev - ery one.
great is God Al - might - y, who has made all things well.

WORDS: Cecil Frances Alexander
MUSIC: 17th cent. English melody

48

Cantemos al Señor
(Let's Sing unto the Lord)

Can - te - mos al Se - ñor un him - no de a - le - grí - a,
un
Let's sing un - to the Lord a hymn of glad re - joic - ing. Let's

cán - ti - co de a - mor al na - cer el nue - vo dí - a.
Él
sing a hymn of love, at the new day's fresh be - gin - ning. God

hi - zo el cie - lo, el mar, el sol y las es - tre - llas
y
made the sky a - bove, the stars, the sun, the o - ceans; and

vio en e - llos bon - dad, pues sus o - bras e - ran be - llas.
God saw it was good, for those works were filled with beau - ty.

Estribillo (Refrain)

¡A - le - lu - ya! ¡A - le - lu - ya! Can -
Al - le - lu - ia! Al - le - lu - ia! Let's

te - mos al Se - ñor. ¡A - le - lu - ya! Can -
sing un - to the Lord. Al - le - lu - ia! Let's

te - mos al Se - ñor. ¡A - le - lu - ya!
sing un - to the Lord. Al - le - lu - ia!

WORDS: Carlos Rosas; trans. Roberto Escamilla, Elise S. Eslinger, and George Lockwood
MUSIC: Carlos Rosas

God, Who Stretched the Spangled Heavens 49

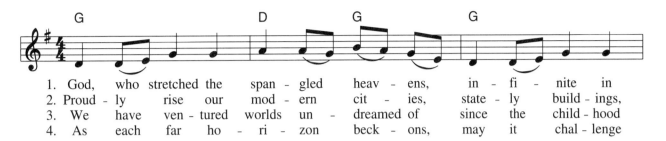

1. God, who stretched the span - gled heav - ens, in - fi - nite in
2. Proud - ly rise our mod - ern cit - ies, state - ly build - ings,
3. We have ven - tured worlds un - dreamed of since the child - hood
4. As each far ho - ri - zon beck - ons, may it chal - lenge

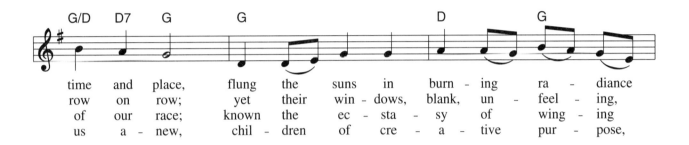

time and place, flung the suns in burn - ing ra - diance
row on row; yet their win - dows, blank, un - feel - ing,
of our race; known the ec - sta - sy of wing - ing
us a - new, chil - dren of cre - a - tive pur - pose,

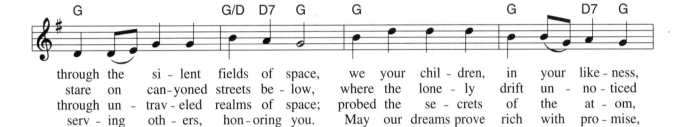

through the si - lent fields of space, we your chil - dren, in your like - ness,
stare on can - yoned streets be - low, where the lone - ly drift un - no - ticed
through un - trav - eled realms of space; probed the se - crets of the at - om,
serv - ing oth - ers, hon - oring you. May our dreams prove rich with pro - mise,

share in - ven - tive powers with you. Great Cre - a - tor,
in the cit - y's ebb and flow, lost to pur - pose
yield - ing un - i - mag - ined power, fac - ing us with
each en - deav - or well be - gun. Great Cre - a - tor,

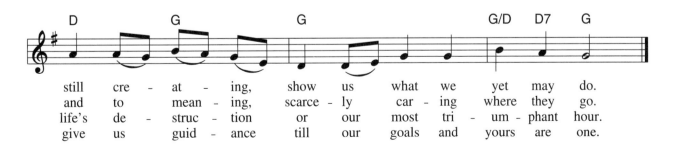

still cre - at - ing, show us what we yet may do.
and to mean - ing, scarce - ly car - ing where they go.
life's de - struc - tion or our most tri - um - phant hour.
give us guid - ance till our goals and yours are one.

WORDS: Catherine Cameron
MUSIC: William Moore
Words © 1967 Hope Publishing Co.

50   I Love to Tell the Story

WORDS: Katherine Hankey
MUSIC: William G. Fischer

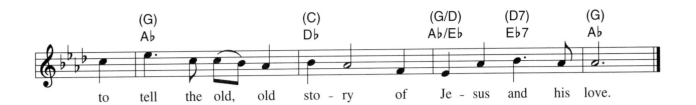

to tell the old, old sto - ry of Je - sus and his love.

All Hail the Power of Jesus' Name

51

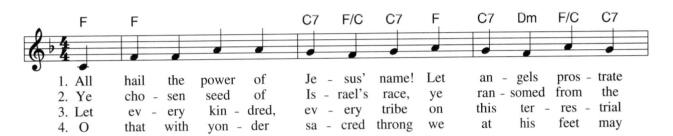

1. All hail the power of Je - sus' name! Let an - gels pros - trate
2. Ye cho - sen seed of Is - rael's race, ye ran - somed from the
3. Let ev - ery kin - dred, ev - ery tribe on this ter - res - trial
4. O that with yon - der sa - cred throng we at his feet may

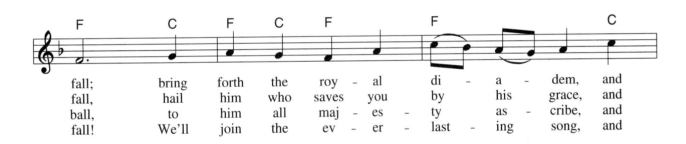

fall; bring forth the roy - al di - a - dem, and
fall, hail him who saves you by his grace, and
ball, to him all maj - es - ty as - cribe, and
fall! We'll join the ev - er - last - ing song, and

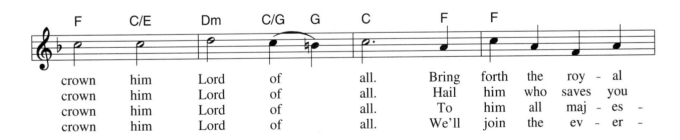

crown him Lord of all. Bring forth the roy - al
crown him Lord of all. Hail him who saves you
crown him Lord of all. To him all maj - es -
crown him Lord of all. We'll join the ev - er -

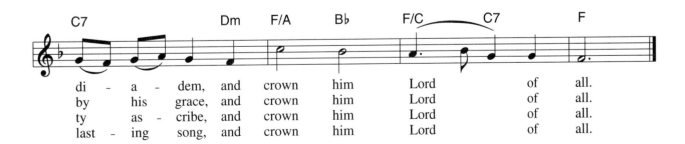

di - a - dem, and crown him Lord of all.
by his grace, and crown him Lord of all.
ty as - cribe, and crown him Lord of all.
last - ing song, and crown him Lord of all.

WORDS: Edward Perronet; alt. John Rippon
MUSIC: Oliver Holden

52   Come, Christians, Join to Sing

1. Come, Chris-tians, join to sing: Al - le - lu - ia! A - men!
2. Come, lift your hearts on high: Al - le - lu - ia! A - men!
3. Praise yet the Lord a - gain: Al - le - lu - ia! A - men!

loud praise to Christ our King: Al - le - lu - ia! A - men!
Let prais - es fill the sky: Al - le - lu - ia! A - men!
Life shall not end the strain: Al - le - lu - ia! A - men!

Let all, with heart and voice, be - fore his throne re - joice;
He is our guide and friend; to us he'll con - de - scend;
On heav - en's bliss - ful shore his good - ness we'll a - dore,

praise is his gra - cious choice: Al - le - lu - ia! A - men!
his love shall nev - er end: Al - le - lu - ia! A - men!
sing - ing for - ev - er - more: Al - le - lu - ia! A - men!

WORDS: Christian Henry Bateman
MUSIC: Trad. melody

Alleluia, Alleluia

Refrain

Al - le - lu - ia, al - le - lu - ia! Give thanks to the

ris - en Lord. Al - le - lu - ia, al - le - lu - ia! Give

praise to his name. *(To Stanzas)* name. *Fine*

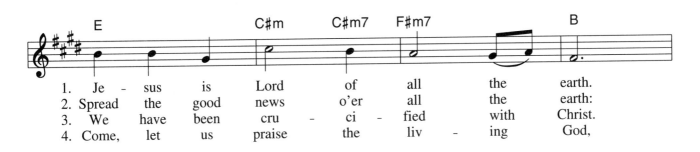

1. Je - sus is Lord of all the earth.
2. Spread the good news o'er all the earth:
3. We have been cru - ci - fied with Christ.
4. Come, let us praise the liv - ing God,

Refrain

He is the King of cre - a - tion.
Je - sus has died and has ris - en.
Now we shall live for - ev - er.
joy - ful - ly sing to our Sav - ior.

Al - le -

WORDS and MUSIC: Donald Fishel

54

O How I Love Jesus

1. There is a name I love to hear, I love to sing its worth; it
2. It tells me of a Sav-ior's love, who died to set me free; it
3. It tells of one whose lov-ing heart can feel my deep-est woe; who

sounds like mu - sic in my ear, the sweet - est name on earth.
tells me of his pre - cious blood, the sin - ner's per - fect plea.
in each sor - row bears a part that none can bear be - low.

Refrain

O how I love Je - sus, O how I love Je - sus,

O how I love Je - sus, be - cause he first loved me!

WORDS: Frederick Whitfield
MUSIC: 19th cent. USA melody

55

Open Our Eyes

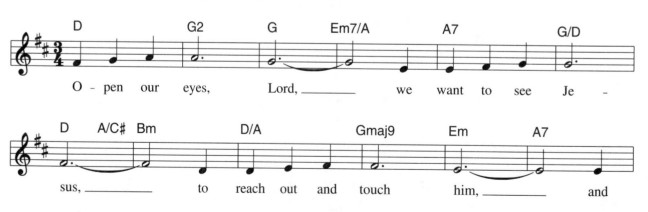

O - pen our eyes, Lord, _____ we want to see Je -

sus, _____ to reach out and touch him, _____ and

WORDS and MUSIC: Bob Cull

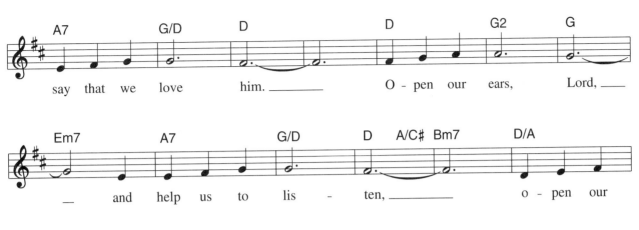

say that we love him. _____ O - pen our ears, Lord, ____

_ and help us to lis - ten, _____ o - pen our

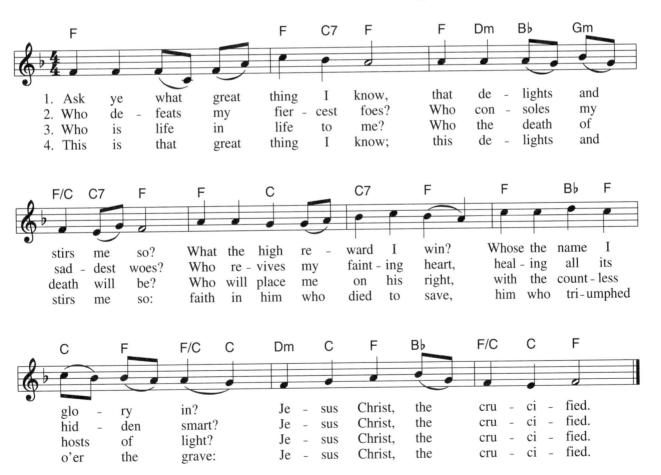

eyes, Lord, _____ we want to see Je - sus.

Ask Ye What Great Thing I Know

56

1. Ask ye what great thing I know, that de - lights and
2. Who de - feats my fier - cest foes? Who con - soles my
3. Who is life in life to me? Who the death of
4. This is that great thing I know; this de - lights and

stirs me so? What the high re - ward I win? Whose the name I
sad - dest woes? Who re - vives my faint - ing heart, heal - ing all its
death will be? Who will place me on his right, with the count - less
stirs me so: faith in him who died to save, him who tri - umphed

glo - ry in? Je - sus Christ, the cru - ci - fied.
hid - den smart? Je - sus Christ, the cru - ci - fied.
hosts of light? Je - sus Christ, the cru - ci - fied.
o'er the grave: Je - sus Christ, the cru - ci - fied.

WORDS: Johann C. Schwedler; trans. Benjamin H. Kennedy
MUSIC: H. A. César Malan

57

My Jesus, I Love Thee

1. My Je - sus, I love thee, I know thou art mine; for
2. I love thee be - cause thou hast first lov - ed me, and
3. In man - sions of glo - ry and end - less de - light, I'll

thee all the fol - lies of sin I re - sign. My
pur - chased my par - don on Cal - va - ry's tree; I
ev - er a - dore thee in heav - en so bright; I'll

gra - cious Re - deem - er, my Sav - ior art thou; if
love thee for wear - ing the thorns on thy brow; if
sing with the glit - ter - ing crown on my brow; if

ev - er I loved thee, my Je - sus, 'tis now.
ev - er I loved thee, my Je - sus, 'tis now.
ev - er I loved thee, my Je - sus, 'tis now.

WORDS: William R. Featherstone
MUSIC: Adoniram J. Gordon

58

His Name Is Wonderful

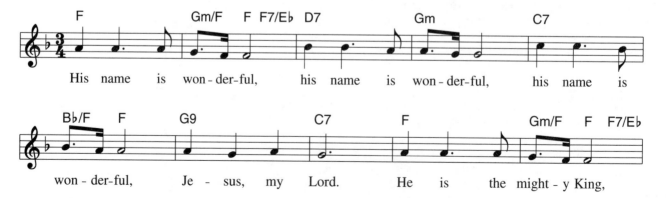

His name is won - der - ful, his name is won - der - ful, his name is

won - der - ful, Je - sus, my Lord. He is the might - y King,

WORDS and MUSIC: Audrey Mieir

Master of ev-ery-thing; his name is won-der-ful, Je - sus, my
Lord. He's the great Shep-herd, the Rock of all a - ges, al-might-y
God is he; _____ bow down be-fore him, love and a -
dore him, his name is won-der-ful, Je - sus, my Lord.

Jesus, the Very Thought of Thee   59

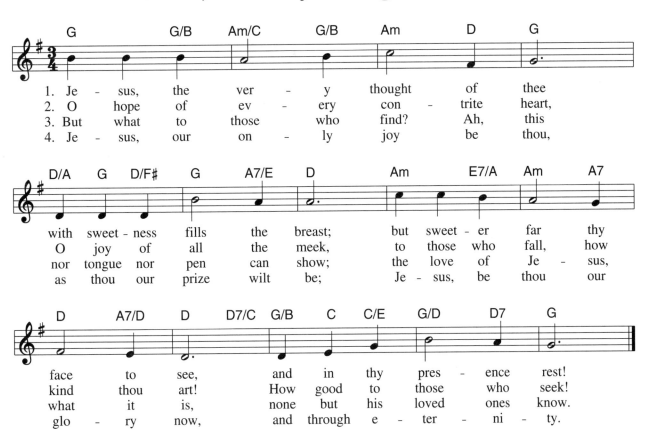

1. Je - sus, the ver - y thought of thee
2. O hope of ev - ery con - trite heart,
3. But what to those who find? Ah, this
4. Je - sus, our on - ly joy be thou,

with sweet - ness fills the breast; but sweet - er far thy
O joy of all the meek, to those who fall, how
nor tongue nor pen can show; the love of Je - sus,
as thou our prize wilt be; Je - sus, be thou our

face to see, and in thy pres - ence rest!
kind thou art! How good to those who seek!
what it is, none but his loved ones know.
glo - ry now, and through e - ter - ni - ty.

WORDS: Attr. to Bernard of Clairvaux, 12th cent.; trans. Edward Caswall
MUSIC: John B. Dykes

60 Majesty, Worship His Majesty

WORDS and MUSIC: Jack Hayford

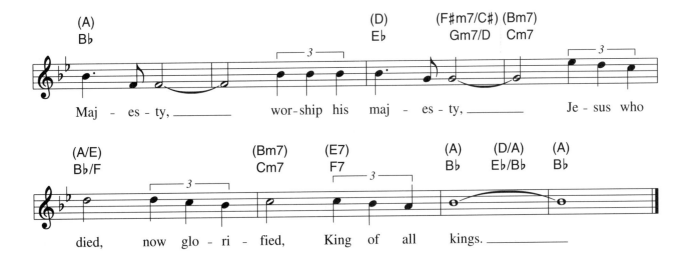

(A)
Bb

(D)
Eb

(F#m7/C#) (Bm7)
Gm7/D Cm7

Maj - es - ty, _____ wor-ship his maj - es - ty, _____ Je - sus who

(A/E)
Bb/F

(Bm7)
Cm7

(E7)
F7

(A)
Bb

(D/A)
Eb/Bb

(A)
Bb

died, now glo - ri - fied, King of all kings. _____

Jesús Es Mi Rey Soberano   61
(O Jesus, My King and My Sovereign)

C   F   C   C   A

Je - sús es mi Rey so - be - ra - no, mi go - zo es can - tar su lo -
O   Je - sus, *my King and my Sov - ereign, my joy is to sing him my*

G7/D   G7   G9   G7

or;   es Rey, y me ve cual her - ma - no, es Rey y me im - par - te su a -
praise. He's king, yet he treats me like fam - ily, he's king, yet he shares all his

C   C   F   C   C9   C7

mor. De - jan - do su tro - no de glo - ria, me vi - no a sa - car de la es -
love. He left all his glo - ry in heav - en to come lift my life from the

F   D#dim7   D7   C/G   D7/G   G7   C

co - ria, y yo soy fe - liz, y yo soy fe - liz por él.
ash - es. I'm hap - py to - day, life's joy came to stay through him.

WORDS: Vicente Mendoza; trans. Esther Frances and George Lockwood
MUSIC: Vicente Mendoza
Trans. © 1982, 1989 The United Methodist Publishing House

62 When Morning Gilds the Skies

1. When morn - ing gilds the skies my heart a - wak - ing
2. The night be - comes as day when from the heart we
3. Let all the earth a - round ring joy - ous with the
4. Be this, while life is mine, my can - ti - cle di -

cries: May Je - sus Christ be praised! A -
say: May Je - sus Christ be praised! The
sound: May Je - sus Christ be praised! In
vine: May Je - sus Christ be praised! Be

like at work and prayer, to Je - sus I re -
powers of dark - ness fear when this sweet chant they
heaven's e - ter - nal bliss the love - liest strain is
this th'e - ter - nal song through all the a - ges

pair: May Je - sus Christ be praised!
hear: May Je - sus Christ be praised!
this: May Je - sus Christ be praised!
long: May Je - sus Christ be praised!

WORDS: *Katholisches Gesangbuch*; sts. 1, 2, 4 trans. Edward Caswall; st. 3 trans. Robert S. Bridges
MUSIC: Joseph Barnby

63 Alleluia

1. Al - le - lu - ia, al - le - lu - ia, al - le -

lu - ia, al - le - lu - ia, al - le - lu - ia, al - le -

WORDS and MUSIC: Jerry Sinclair

lu - ia, al - le - lu - ia, al - le - lu - ia.

2. He's my Savior
3. I will praise him

Fairest Lord Jesus

1. Fair - est Lord Je - sus, rul - er of all
2. Fair are the mead - ows, fair - er still the
3. Fair is the sun - shine, fair - er still the
4. Beau - ti - ful Sav - ior! Lord of all the

na - ture, O thou of God and man the
wood - lands, robed in the bloom - ing garb of
moon - light, and all the twink - ling star - ry
na - tions! Son of God and Son of

Son, thee will I cher - ish, thee will I
spring: Je - sus is fair - er, Je - sus is
host: Je - sus shines bright - er, Je - sus shines
Man! Glo - ry and hon - or, praise, ad - o -

hon - or, thou, my soul's glo - ry, joy, and crown.
pur - er, who makes the woe - ful heart to sing.
pur - er than all the an - gels heaven can boast.
ra - tion, now and for - ev - er - more be thine.

WORDS: *Münster Gesangbuch*; trans. Joseph August Seiss
MUSIC: *Schlesische Volkslieder*

65

Who Is He in Yonder Stall

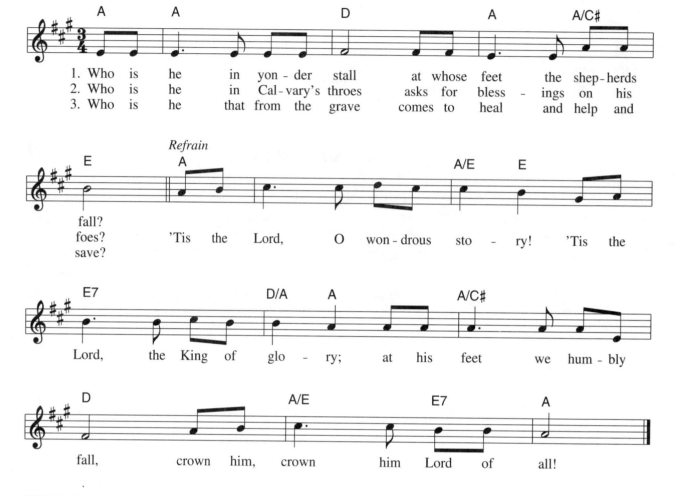

1. Who is he in yon-der stall at whose feet the shep-herds
2. Who is he in Cal-vary's throes asks for bless – ings on his
3. Who is he that from the grave comes to heal and help and

Refrain

fall?
foes? 'Tis the Lord, O won-drous sto – ry! 'Tis the
save?

Lord, the King of glo – ry; at his feet we hum – bly

fall, crown him, crown him Lord of all!

WORDS and MUSIC: Benjamin R. Hanby

66

Jesus Loves Me

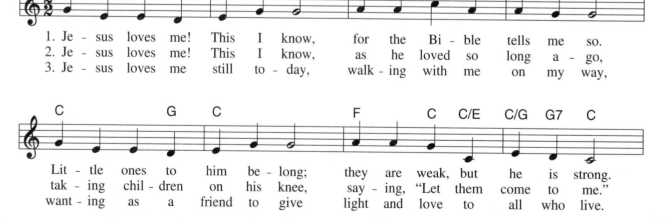

1. Je – sus loves me! This I know, for the Bi – ble tells me so.
2. Je – sus loves me! This I know, as he loved so long a – go,
3. Je – sus loves me still to – day, walk-ing with me on my way,

Lit – tle ones to him be – long; they are weak, but he is strong.
tak-ing chil – dren on his knee, say – ing, "Let them come to me."
want – ing as a friend to give light and love to all who live.

WORDS: St. 1 Anna B. Warner; sts. 2-3 David Rutherford McGuire
MUSIC: William B. Bradbury

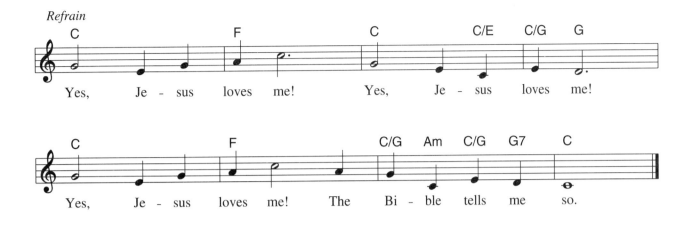

Refrain

Yes, Je - sus loves me! Yes, Je - sus loves me!

Yes, Je - sus loves me! The Bi - ble tells me so.

Jesus Be Praised

67

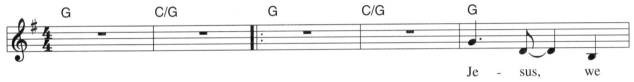

Je - sus, we

wor - ship you, with our voic - es filled with prais - es, Je - sus, we

wor - ship you; songs of love we raise. Je - sus,

Je - sus be praised! _____ Je - sus, Je - sus be

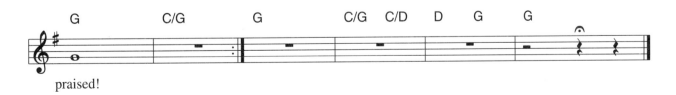

praised!

WORDS and MUSIC: Handt Hanson

68 Shine, Jesus, Shine

Refrain

Shine, Jesus, shine, __ fill this land with the Father's glory,
blaze, Spirit, blaze, __ set our hearts on fire;
flow, river, flow, __ flood the nations with grace and mercy,
send forth your word, __ Lord, and let there be light.

1. Lord, the light of your love is shining in the midst of the
2. Lord, I come to your awesome presence from the shadows in-
3. As we gaze on your kingly brightness, so our faces dis-

darkness shining; Jesus, Light of the World, shine upon us,
to your radiance; by the blood I may enter your brightness,
play your likeness; ever changing from glory to glory,

set us free by the truth you now bring us.
search me, try me, consume all my darkness. Shine on
mirrored here may our lives tell your story.

WORDS and MUSIC: Graham Kendrick

Alleluia

69

WORDS and MUSIC: Cathy Townley

© 1997 Abingdon Press

70   There's Something About That Name

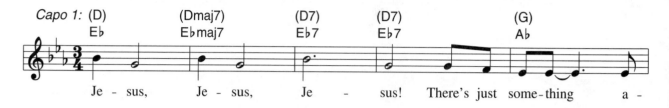

Je - sus, Je - sus, Je - sus! There's just some - thing a -

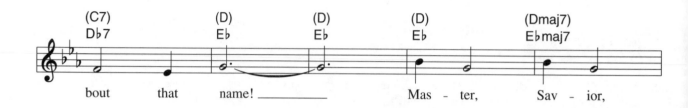

bout that name! _____ Mas - ter, Sav - ior,

Je - sus! Like the fra - grance af - ter the rain. _____

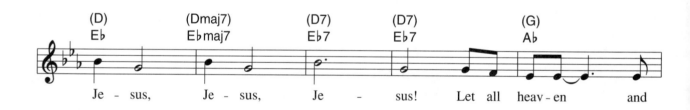

Je - sus, Je - sus, Je - sus! Let all heav - en and

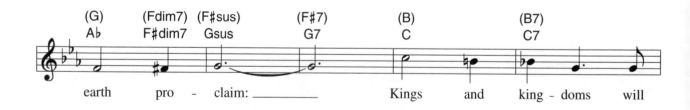

earth pro - claim: _____ Kings and king - doms will

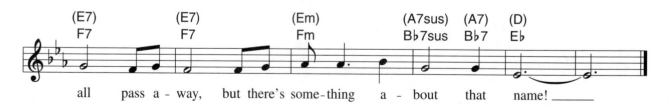

all pass a - way, but there's some - thing a - bout that name! _____

WORDS: Gloria Gaither and William J. Gaither
MUSIC: William J. Gaither

Lord, I Lift Your Name on High

WORDS and MUSIC: Rick Founds

As the Deer

72

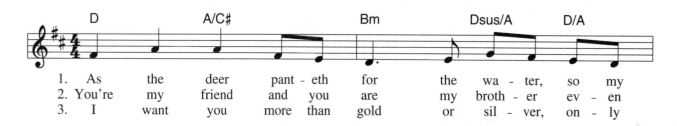

1. As the deer pant - eth for the wa - ter, so my
2. You're my friend and you are my broth - er ev - en
3. I want you more than gold or sil - ver, on - ly

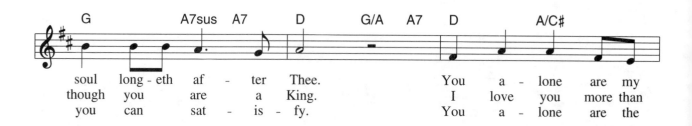

soul long - eth af - ter Thee. You a - lone are my
though you are a King. I love you more than
you can sat - is - fy. You a - lone are the

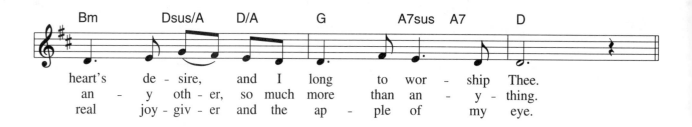

heart's de - sire, and I long to wor - ship Thee.
an - y oth - er, so much more than an - y - thing.
real joy - giv - er and the ap - ple of my eye.

Refrain

You a - lone are my strength, my shield; to you a - lone may my

spir - it yield. You a - lone are my

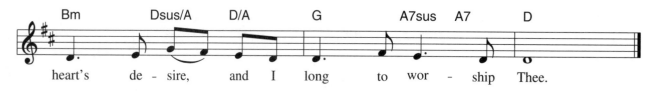

heart's de - sire, and I long to wor - ship Thee.

WORDS and MUSIC: Martin Nystrom

Emmanuel, Emmanuel

73

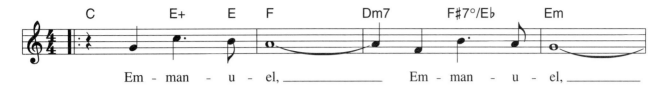

Em - man - u - el, _____ Em - man - u - el, _____

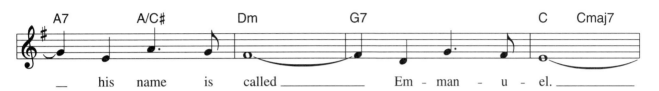

_ his name is called _____ Em - man - u - el. _____

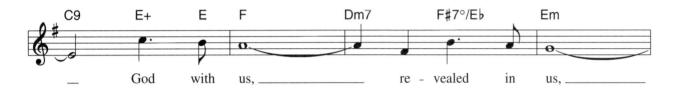

_ God with us, _____ re - vealed in us, _____

_ his name is called _____ Em - man - u - el. _____

WORDS and MUSIC: Bob McGee

Prepare the Way of the Lord

74

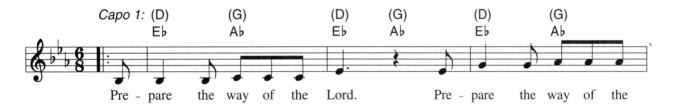

Pre - pare the way of the Lord.   Pre - pare the way of the

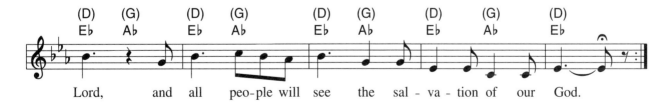

Lord,   and all peo-ple will see the sal - va - tion of our God.

WORDS: Isaiah 40:3; 52:10

MUSIC: Jacques Berthier and the Community of Taizé

75

Come, Thou Long-Expected Jesus

1. Come, thou long-ex-pect-ed Je-sus, born to
2. Born thy peo-ple to de-liv-er, born a

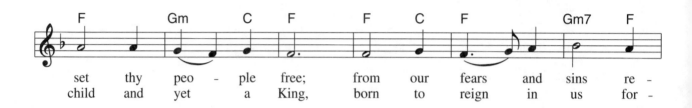

set thy peo-ple free; from our fears and sins re-
child and yet a King, born to reign in us for-

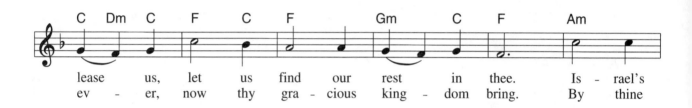

lease us, let us find our rest in thee. Is-rael's
ev-er, now thy gra-cious king-dom bring. By thine

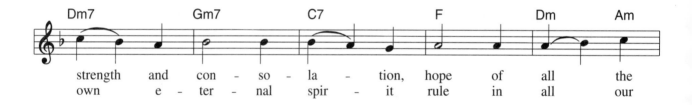

strength and con-so-la-tion, hope of all the
own e-ter-nal spir-it rule in all our

earth thou art; dear de-sire of ev-ery
hearts a-lone; by thine all suf-fi-cient

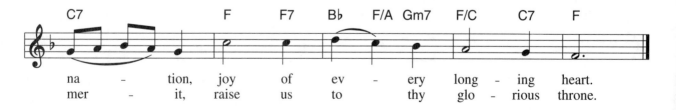

na-tion, joy of ev-ery long-ing heart.
mer-it, raise us to thy glo-rious throne.

WORDS: Charles Wesley
MUSIC: Rowland H. Prichard

O Come, O Come, Emmanuel

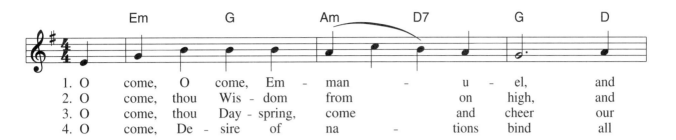

1. O come, O come, Em - man - u - el, and
2. O come, thou Wis - dom from on high, and
3. O come, thou Day - spring, come and cheer our
4. O come, De - sire of na - tions bind all

ran - som cap - tive Is - ra - el, that
or - der all things far and nigh; to
spir - its by thy jus - tice here; dis -
peo - ples in one heart and mind. From

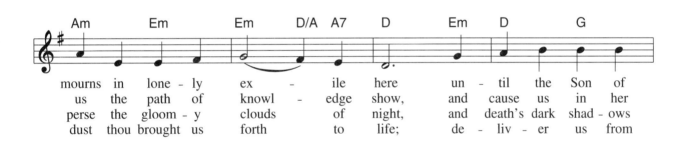

mourns in lone - ly ex - ile here un - til the Son of
us the path of knowl - edge show, and cause us in her
perse the gloom - y clouds of night, and death's dark shad - ows
dust thou brought us forth to life; de - liv - er us from

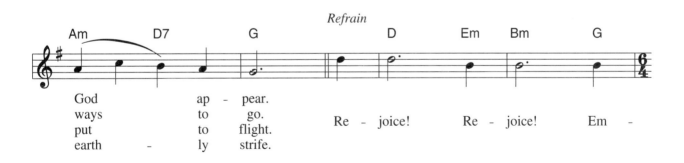

Refrain

God ap - pear.
ways to go.
put to flight.   Re - joice! Re - joice! Em -
earth - ly strife.

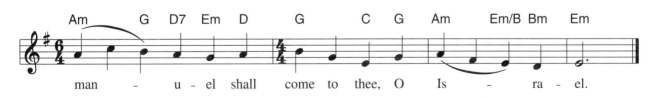

man - u - el shall come to thee, O Is - ra - el.

WORDS: 9th cent. Latin; trans. sts. 1, 6cd, 7ab, *The Hymnal 1940*; st. 2, Henry Sloane Coffin; sts. 6ab, 7cd, Laurence Hull Stookey
MUSIC: 15th cent. French

77

Blessed Be the God of Israel

1. Blessed be the God of Is - rael, who comes to set us free, who visits and re - deems us, and grants us lib - er - ty. The proph - ets spoke of mer - cy, of free - dom and re - lease; God shall ful - fill the prom - ise to bring our peo - ple peace.

2. Now from the house of Da - vid a child of grace is given; a Sav - ior comes a - mong us to raise us up to heaven. Be - fore him goes the her - ald, fore - run - ner in the way, the proph - et of sal - va - tion, the har - bin - ger of day.

3. On pris - on - ers of dark - ness the sun be - gins to rise, the dawn - ing of for - give - ness up - on the sin - er's eyes, to guide the feet of pil - grims a - long the paths of peace; O bless our God and Sav - ior with songs that nev - er cease!

WORDS: Michael Perry
MUSIC: Hal H. Hopson

Words © 1973 Hope Publishing Co.; music © 1983 Hope Publishing Co.

78

Toda la Tierra
(All Earth Is Waiting)

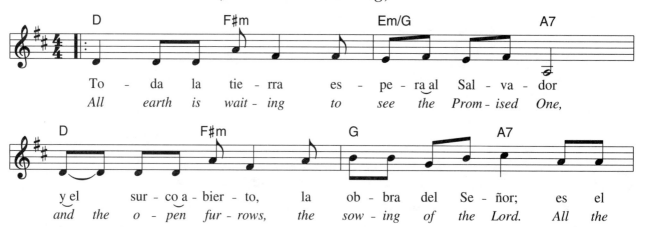

To - da la tie - rra es - pe - ra al Sal - va - dor
All earth is wait - ing to see the Prom - ised One,

y el sur - co a - bier - to, la ob - ra del Se - ñor; es el
and the o - pen fur - rows, the sow - ing of the Lord. All the

WORDS: Catalonian text by Alberto Taulé; English trans. Gertrude C. Suppe
MUSIC: Alberto Taulé

© 1972 Alberto Taulé; trans. © 1989 The United Methodist Publishing House

mun - do que lu - cha por la li - ber - tad, re -
world, *bound and strug - gling,* *seeks* *true* *lib - er - ty;* *it*

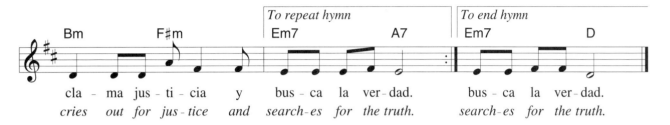

To repeat hymn Em7 A7 | *To end hymn* Em7 D

cla - ma jus - ti - cia y bus - ca la ver - dad. bus - ca la ver - dad.
cries *out for jus - tice* *and* *search - es* *for* *the truth.* *search - es* *for* *the truth.*

Away in a Manger

79

Capo 3: (D)   (G)   (D)
F   B♭   F

1. A - way in a man - ger, no crib for a bed,
2. The cat - tle are low - ing, the ba - by a - wakes,
3. Be near me, Lord Je - sus, I ask thee to stay

(A7)   (G/D) (D)   (D)
C7   B♭/F F   F

the lit - tle Lord Je - sus laid down his sweet head.
but lit - tle Lord Je - sus, no cry - ing he makes;
close by me for - ev - er, and love me, I pray;

(D)   (G)   (D)
F   B♭   F

The stars in the sky looked down where he lay,
I love thee, Lord Je - sus, look down from the sky
bless all the dear chil - dren in thy ten - der care,

(A7)   (D)   (Em)   (A7) (D)
C7   F   Gm   C7   F

the lit - tle Lord Je - sus, a - sleep on the hay.
and stay by my cra - dle till morn - ing is nigh.
and fit us for heav - en to live with thee there.

WORDS: Anonymous
MUSIC: James R. Murray

80   What Child Is This

1. What child is this who, laid to rest, on Mary's lap is
2. Why lies he in such mean es - tate where ox and ass are
3. So bring him in - cense, gold, and myrrh, come, peas - ant, king, to

sleep - ing? Whom an - gels greet with an - thems sweet, while
feed - ing? Good Chris - tians, fear, for sin - ners here the
own him; the King of kings sal - va - tion brings, let

Refrain

shep - herds watch are keep - ing?
si - lent Word is plead - ing.   This, this is Christ the King, whom
lov - ing hearts en - throne him.

shep - herds guard and an - gels sing; haste, haste to

bring him laud, the babe, the son of Ma - ry.

WORDS: William C. Dix
MUSIC: 16th cent. English melody

81   In the Bleak Midwinter

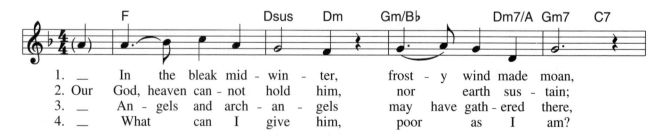

1. _ In the bleak mid - win - ter, frost - y wind made moan,
2. Our God, heaven can - not hold him, nor earth sus - tain;
3. _ An - gels and arch - an - gels may have gath - ered there,
4. _ What can I give him, poor as I am?

WORDS: Christina G. Rossetti
MUSIC: Gustav Holst

Infant Holy, Infant Lowly   **82**

earth stood hard as i - ron, wa - ter like a stone;
heaven and earth shall flee a - way when he comes to reign.
cher - u - bim and ser - a - phim throng - ed the air;
If I were a shep - herd, I would bring a lamb;

snow had fall - en, snow on snow, snow on snow, _
In the bleak mid - win - ter a sta - ble place suf - ficed the
but his moth - er on - ly, in her maid - en bliss, _
if I were a Wise Man, I would do my part; yet

in the bleak mid - win - ter, long a - go.
Lord God Al - might - y, Je - sus Christ.
wor - shiped the be - lov - ed with a kiss
what I can I give him: give my heart.

1. In - fant ho - ly, in - fant low - ly, for his bed a cat - tle
2. Flocks were sleep - ing, shep-herds keep - ing vig - il till the morn - ing

stall; ox - en low - ing, lit - tle know - ing, Christ the babe is Lord of
new saw the glo - ry, heard the sto - ry, tid - ings of a gos - pel

all. Swift are wing - ing an - gels sing - ing, no - els ring - ing, tid - ings
true. Thus re - joic - ing, free from sor - row, prais - es voic - ing, greet the

bring - ing: Christ the babe is Lord of all.   *(Interlude, ending)*
mor - row: Christ the babe was born for you.

WORDS: Polish carol; trans. Edith M. G. Reed
MUSIC: Polish carol

83

Niño Lindo
(Child So Lovely)

Refrain

Ni - ño lin - do, an - te ti me rin - do,
Child so love - ly, here I kneel be - fore you,

ni - ño lin - do, e - res tú mi Dios.
child so love - ly, you are Christ my God.

Ni - ño lin - do, an - te ti me rin - do;
Child so love - ly, here I kneel be - fore you,

ni - ño lin - do, e - res tú mi Dios. Dios.
child so love - ly, you are Christ the Lord. Lord.

E - sa - tu her - mo - su - ra; e - se tu can - dor, el al - ma me
You have heav-en's beau - ty, and God's pu - ri - ty, steal-ing my de-

ro - ba, el al - ma me ro - ba, me ro - ba el a - mor.
vo - tion, steal-ing my af - fec - tion, steal-ing all my soul.

WORDS: Trad. Venezuelan; trans. George Lockwood
MUSIC: Trad. Venezuelan melody

He Is Born

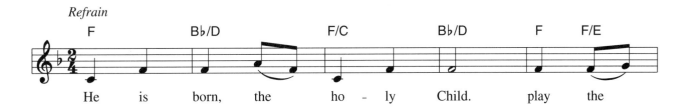

Refrain

He is born, the ho - ly Child. play the

o - boe and bag - pipes mer - ri - ly! He is born, the

ho - ly Child, sing we all of the Sav - ior mild.

Fine

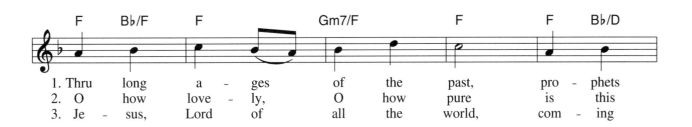

1. Thru long a - ges of the past, pro - phets
2. O how love - ly, O how pure is this
3. Je - sus, Lord of all the world, com - ing

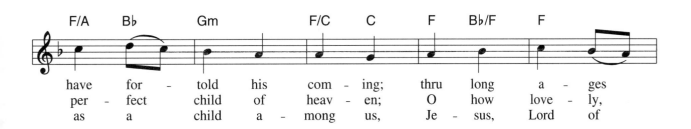

have for - told his com - ing; thru long a - ges
per - fect child of heav - en; O how love - ly,
as a child a - mong us, Je - sus, Lord of

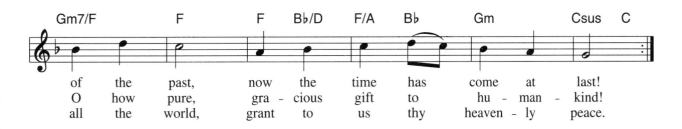

of the past, now the time has come at last!
O how pure, gra - cious gift to hu - man - kind!
all the world, grant to us thy heaven - ly peace.

WORDS: Trad. 19th cent. French carol; trans. anonymous
MUSIC: 18th cent. French carol

85   O Come, All Ye Faithful

1. O come, all ye faith - ful, joy - ful and tri - um - phant, O
2. __ Sing, choirs of an - gels, sing in ex - ul - ta - tion; O
3. __ Yea, Lord, we greet thee, born this hap - py morn - ing, __

come ye, O come ye, to Beth - le - hem.
sing, all ye cit - i - zens of heaven a - bove!
Je - sus, to thee be all glo - ry given.

Come and be - hold him, born the King of an - gels;
Glo - ry to God, all glo - ry in the high - est;
Word of the Fa - ther, now in flesh ap - pear - ing:

Refrain

O come, let us a - dore him, O come, let us a - dore him,

O come, let us a - dore him, Christ the Lord.

WORDS: John F. Wade; trans. Frederick Oakeley and others
MUSIC: John F. Wade

86   Sing We Now of Christmas

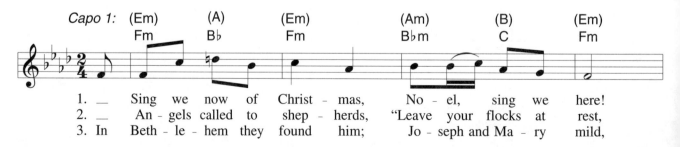

1. __ Sing we now of Christ - mas, No - el, sing we here!
2. __ An - gels called to shep - herds, "Leave your flocks at rest,
3. In Beth - le - hem they found him; Jo - seph and Ma - ry mild,

WORDS and MUSIC: Trad. French Carol

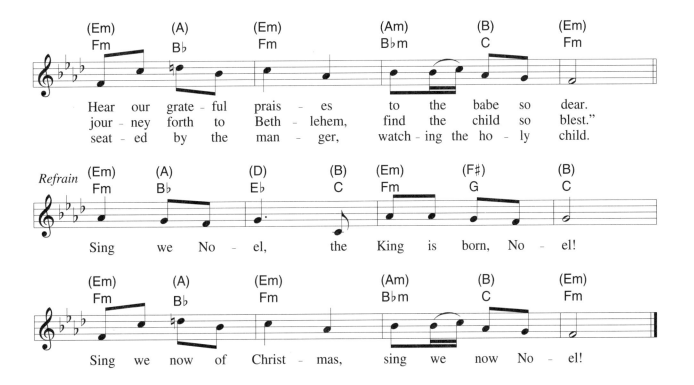

Hear our grate-ful prais - es to the babe so dear.
jour - ney forth to Beth - lehem, find the child so blest."
seat - ed by the man - ger, watch - ing the ho - ly child.

Refrain

Sing we No - el, the King is born, No - el!

Sing we now of Christ - mas, sing we now No - el!

Silent Night, Holy Night 87

1. Si - lent night, ho - ly night, all is calm, all is bright
2. Si - lent night, ho - ly night, shep - herds quake at the sight;
3. Si - lent night, ho - ly night, Son of God, love's pure light;
4. Si - lent night, ho - ly night, won - drous star, lend thy light;

round yon vir - gin moth - er and child. Ho - ly in - fant, so ten - der and mild,
glo - ries stream from heav - en a - far, heaven - ly hosts sing Al - le - lu - ia!
ra - diant beams from thy ho - ly face with the dawn of re - deem - ing grace,
with the an - gels let us sing, Al - le - lu - ia to our King;

sleep in heav - en - ly peace, sleep in heav - en - ly peace.
Christ the Sav - ior is born, Christ the Sav - ior is born!
Je - sus, Lord, at thy birth, Je - sus, Lord, at thy birth.
Christ the Sav - ior is born, Christ the Sav - ior is born!

WORDS: Joseph Mohr, alt.; sts. 1, 2, 3 trans. John F. Young; st. 4 trans. anonymous
MUSIC: Franz Gruber

88 The Friendly Beasts

1. Je - sus, our broth - er, strong and good, was
2. "I," said the don - key, shag - gy and brown, "I
3. "I," said the sheep with curl - y horn, "I
4. Thus all the beasts, by some good spell, in the

hum - bly born in a sta - ble rude, and the
car - ried his moth - er up - hill and down, I
gave him my wool for his blan - ket warm, he
sta - ble dark were glad to tell of the

friend - ly beasts a - round him stood,
car - ried his moth - er to Beth - le - hem town;
wore my coat on Christ - mas morn;
gifts they gave Em - man - u - el,

Je - sus, our broth - er, strong and good.
I," said the don - key, shag - gy and brown.
I," said the sheep with curl - y horn.
the gifts they gave Em - man - u - el.

WORDS: 12th cent. French carol; trans. anonymous
MUSIC: Medieval French melody

89 That Boy-Child of Mary

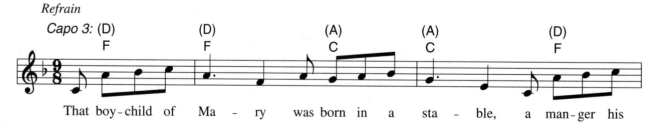

Refrain
Capo 3: (D) (D) (A) (A) (D)

That boy-child of Ma - ry was born in a sta - ble, a man-ger his

WORDS: Tom Colvin
MUSIC: Trad. Malawi melody; adapt. Tom Colvin

Go, Tell It on the Mountain

90

1. What shall we call him, child of the
2. His name is Je - sus, God ev - er
3. Gift of the Fa - ther, to hu - man
4. Glad - ly we praise him, love and a -

cra - dle in Beth - le - hem.

man - ger? What name is giv - en in Beth - le - hem?
with us, God giv - en for us in Beth - le - hem.
moth - er, makes him our broth - er of Beth - le - hem.
dore him, give our - selves to him of Beth - le - hem.

Refrain

Go, tell it on the moun - tain, o - ver the hills and ev - ery - where;

Fine

Go, tell it on the moun - tain, that Je - sus Christ is born.

1. While shep - herds kept their watch - ing o'er si - lent flocks by night,
2. The shep - herds feared and trem - bled, when lo! a - bove the earth,
3. Down in a low - ly man - ger the hum - ble Christ was born,

be - hold through - out the heav - ens there shown a ho - ly light.
rang out the an - gel cho - rus that hailed the Sav - ior's birth.
and God sent us sal - va - tion that bless - ed Christ - mas morn.

D.C.

WORDS: African American spiritual; adapt. John W. Work, Jr.
MUSIC: African American spiritual; adapt. William Farley Smith
Adapt. © 1989 The United Methodist Publishing House

91   Joy to the World

WORDS: Isaac Watts
MUSIC: Arr. from G. F. Handel by Lowell Mason

There's a Song in the Air

WORDS: Josiah G. Holland
MUSIC: Karl P. Harrington

93   Hark! the Herald Angels Sing

WORDS: Charles Wesley; alt. by George Whitefield, and others
MUSIC: Felix Mendelssohn

We Three Kings

1. We three kings of O - ri - ent are; bear - ing
2. Born a King on Beth - le - hem's plain, gold I
3. Frank - in - cense to of - fer have I; in - cense
4. Myrrh is mine; its bit - ter per - fume breathes a
5. Glo - rious now be - hold him a - rise; King and

gifts we tra - verse a - far, field and foun - tain, moor and
bring to crown him a - gain, King for - ev - er, ceas - ing
owns a De - i - ty nigh; prayer and prais - ing, voic - es
life of gath - er - ing gloom; sor - rowing, sigh - ing, bleed - ing,
God and sac - ri - fice: Al - le - lu - ia, Al - le -

moun - tain, fol - low - ing yon - der star. _____
nev - er, o - ver us all to reign. _____
rais - ing, wor - ship - ing God on high. _____
dy - ing, sealed in the stone - cold tomb. _____
lu - ia, sounds through the earth and skies. _____

Refrain

O _____ star of won - der, star of light,

star with roy - al beau - ty bright, west - ward lead - ing,

still pro - ceed - ing, guide us to thy per - fect light.

WORDS and MUSIC: John H. Hopkins, Jr.

95

De Tierra Lejana Venimos
(From a Distant Home)

De tie-rra le-ja-na ve-ni-mos a ver-te, nos sir-ve de
From a dis-tant home the Sav-ior we come seek - ing, us-ing as our

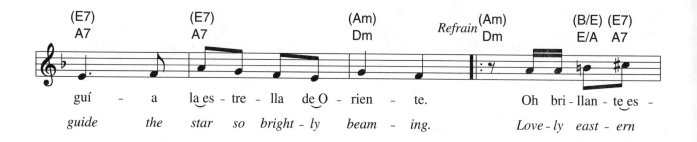

guí - a la es-tre-lla de O-rien - te. Oh bri-llan-te es -
guide the star so bright - ly beam - ing. Love - ly east - ern

tre - lla que a-nun-cias la au-ro - ra no nos fal - te nun - ca
star that tells us of God's morn - ing, heav-en's won-drous light, O

tu luz bien-he-cho-ra.   tu luz bien-he-cho - ra.
nev - er cease thy shin - ing!   *nev - er cease thy shin - ing!*

WORDS: Trad. Puerto Rican carol; trans. George K. Evans
MUSIC: Trad. Puerto Rican carol

Trans. © 1963, 1980 Walter Ehret and George K. Evans, by permission of Walton Music Corp.

The First One Ever

WORDS and MUSIC: Linda Wilberger Egan; alt.

97 When Jesus the Healer Passed Through Galilee

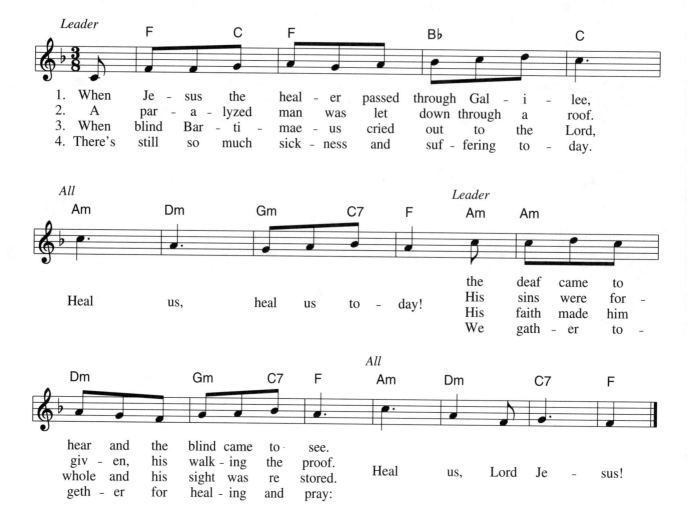

1. When Jesus the healer passed through Galilee,
2. A paralyzed man was let down through a roof.
3. When blind Bartimaeus cried out to the Lord,
4. There's still so much sickness and suffering today.

Heal us, heal us today!

    the deaf came to
    His sins were for-
    His faith made him
    We gather to-

hear and the blind came to see.
given, his walking the proof.
whole and his sight was restored.
gether for healing and pray:

Heal us, Lord Jesus!

WORDS and MUSIC: Peter D. Smith

© 1978 Stainer and Bell, Ltd. and Methodist Church (UK) Div. of Education & Youth (Admin. by Hope Publishing Co.)

98 The Lord's Prayer

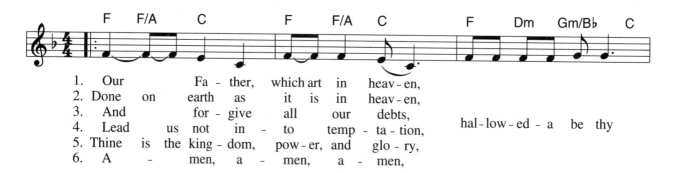

1. Our Father, which art in heaven,
2. Done on earth as it is in heaven,
3. And forgive all our debts,
4. Lead us not into temptation,
5. Thine is the kingdom, power, and glory,
6. Amen, amen, amen,

hallowed a be thy

WORDS: Matthew 6:9-13; adapt. J. Jefferson Cleveland and Verolga Nix
MUSIC: West Indian folk tune

Adapt. © 1981 Abingdon Press

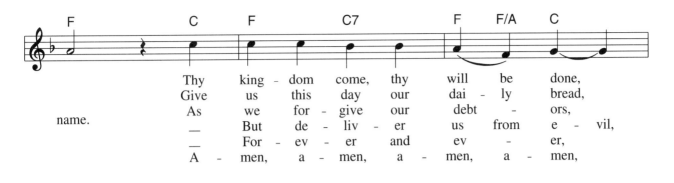

Thy king - dom come, thy will be done,
Give us this day our dai - ly bread,
As we for - give our debt - ors,
— But de - liv - er us from e - vil,
— For - ev - er and ev - er,
A - men, a - men, a - men, a - men,

name.

hal - low - ed - a be thy name. name.

Jesus' Hands Were Kind Hands 99

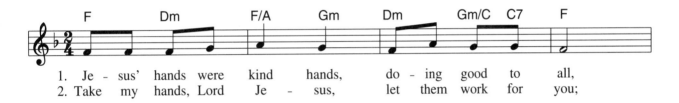

1. Je - sus' hands were kind hands, do - ing good to all,
2. Take my hands, Lord Je - sus, let them work for you;

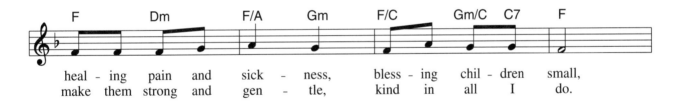

heal - ing pain and sick - ness, bless - ing chil - dren small,
make them strong and gen - tle, kind in all I do.

wash - ing tir - ed feet, and sav - ing those who fall;
Let me watch you, Je - sus, till I'm gen - tle too,

Je - sus' hands were kind hands, do - ing good to all.
till my hands are kind hands, quick to work for you.

WORDS: Margaret Cropper
MUSIC: Old French melody

100 Lord of the Dance

WORDS: Sydney Carter
MUSIC: 19th cent. Shaker tune; adapt. Sydney Carter

Mantos y Palmas
(Filled with Excitement)

101

Man - tos y pal - mas es - par - cien - do, va el pue - blo a - le - gre de Je -
Filled with ex - cite - ment, all the hap - py throng spread cloaks and branch - es on the

ru - sa - lén. A - llá a lo le - jos se em - pie - za a mi - rar
cit - y streets. There in the dis - tance they be - gin to see,

Estribillo (Refrain)

en un po - lli - no al Hi - jo de Dios. Mien - tras mil vo - ces re -
rid - ing on a don - key, comes the Son of God. From ev - ery cor - ner a

sue - nan por do - quier; ho - san - na al que vie - ne en el nom - bre del Se - ñor.
thou - sand voic - es sing prais - es to him who comes in the name of God.

Con un a - lien - to de gran ex - cla - ma - ción pro - rrum - pen con voz triun -
With one great shout of ac - cla - ma - tion loud tri - um - phant song breaks

fal: "¡Ho - san - na! ¡Ho - san - na al Rey!"
forth: "Ho - san - na, ho - san - na to the King!

"¡Ho - san - na! ¡Ho - san - na al Rey!"
Ho - san - na, ho - san - na to the King!"

WORDS: Rubén Ruiz Avila; trans. Gertrude C. Suppe
MUSIC: Rubén Ruiz Avila
© 1972, 1979, 1989 The United Methodist Publishing House

102 Tell Me the Stories of Jesus

1. Tell me the stories of Jesus I love to hear;
2. First let me hear how the children stood round his knee,
3. In-to the city I'd follow the children's band,

things I would ask him to tell me if he were here:
and I shall fancy his blessing resting on me;
waving a branch of the palm tree high in my hand;

scenes by the wayside, tales of the sea,
words full of kindness, deeds full of grace,
one of his heralds, yes, I would sing

stories of Jesus, tell them to me.
all in the lovelight of Jesus' face.
loudest hosannas, "Jesus is King!"

WORDS: William H. Parker
MUSIC: Frederick A. Challinor

103 Hosanna! Hosanna!

Rock (♩ = 160)

Capo 3: (D) F   (G) B♭   (D) F   (G) B♭   (D) F

1. Je-sus rode in-to Je-ru-sa-lem. Ho-san-na! Ho-
2. Ev-ery-bod-y brought their hopes and dreams. Ho-san-na! Ho-

WORDS and MUSIC: Cathy Townley
© 1993 Wellsprings Unlimited, Inc.

104
Were You There

WORDS and MUSIC: African American spiritual; adapt. by William Farley Smith
Adapt. © 1989 The United Methodist Publishing House

What Wondrous Love Is This

1. What won - drous love is this, O my soul, O my
2. What won - drous love is this, O my soul, O my
3. To God and to the Lamb, I will sing, I will
4. And when from death I'm free, I'll sing on, I'll sing

soul, what won - drous love is this, O my soul! What
soul, what won - drous love is this, O my soul! What
sing, to God and to the Lamb, I will sing; to
on, and when from death I'm free, I'll sing on; and

won - drous love is this that caused the Lord of
won - drous love is this that caused the Lord of
God and to the Lamb who is the great I
when from death I'm free, I'll sing and joy - ful

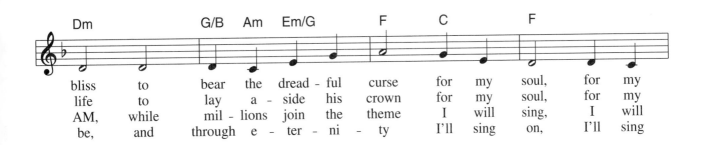

bliss to bear the dread - ful curse for my soul, for my
life to lay a - side his crown for my soul, for my
AM, while mil - lions join the theme I will sing, I will
be, and through e - ter - ni - ty I'll sing on, I'll sing

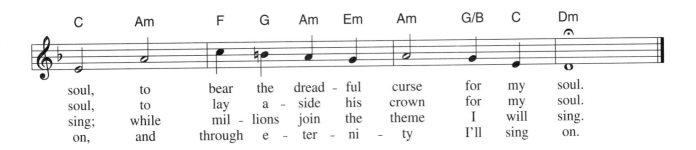

soul, to bear the dread - ful curse for my soul.
soul, to lay a - side his crown for my soul.
sing; while mil - lions join the theme I will sing.
on, and through e - ter - ni - ty I'll sing on.

WORDS and MUSIC: USA folk hymn

106

Alas! and Did My Savior Bleed

1. Alas! and did my Savior bleed, and did my
2. Was it for crimes that I have done, he groaned up-
3. Thus might I hide my blush-ing face while his dear
4. But drops of grief can ne'er re-pay the debt of

Sov-ereign die? _____ Would he de-vote that sa-cred
on the tree? _____ A-maz-ing pit-y! Grace un-
cross ap-pears; _____ dis-solve my heart in thank-ful-
love I owe. _____ Here Lord, I give my-self a-

head for sin - ners such as I? _____
known! And love be - yond de - gree! _____
ness, and melt mine eyes to tears. _____
way; 'tis all that I can do. _____

WORDS: Isaac Watts
MUSIC: Attr. to Hugh Wilson

107

In the Cross of Christ I Glory

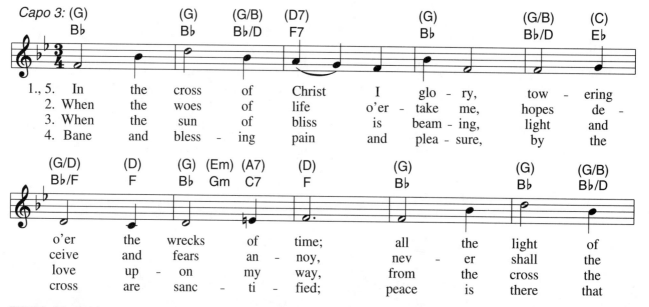

1., 5. In the cross of Christ I glo - ry, tow - ering
2. When the woes of life o'er - take me, hopes de -
3. When the sun of bliss is beam - ing, light and
4. Bane and bless - ing pain and plea - sure, by the

o'er the wrecks of time; all the light of
ceive and fears an - noy, nev - er shall the
love up - on my way, from the cross the
cross are sanc - ti - fied; peace is there that

WORDS: John Bowring
MUSIC: Ithamar Conkey

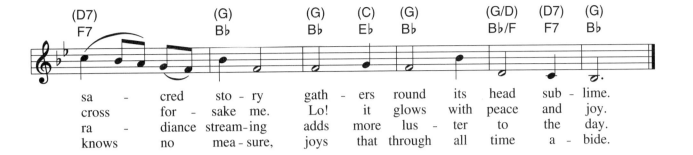

sa - cred sto - ry gath - ers round its head sub - lime.
cross for - sake me. Lo! it glows with peace and joy.
ra - diance stream-ing adds more lus - ter to the day.
knows no mea - sure, joys that through all time a - bide.

When I Survey the Wondrous Cross 108

Capo 3: (D)

1. When I sur - vey the won - drous cross
2. For - bid it, Lord, that I should boast,
3. See, from his head, his hands, his feet,
4. Were the whole realm of na - ture mine,

on which the Prince of Glo - ry died,
save in the death of Christ, my God;
sor - row and love flow min - gled down.
that were an of - fering far too small;

my rich - est gain I count but loss,
all the vain things that charm me most,
Did e'er such love and sor - row meet,
love so a - maz - ing, so di - vine,

and pour con - tempt on all my pride.
I sac - ri - fice them to his blood.
or thorns com - pose so rich a crown?
de - mands my soul, my life, my all.

WORDS: Isaac Watts
MUSIC: Lowell Mason

109   Jesus, Keep Me Near the Cross

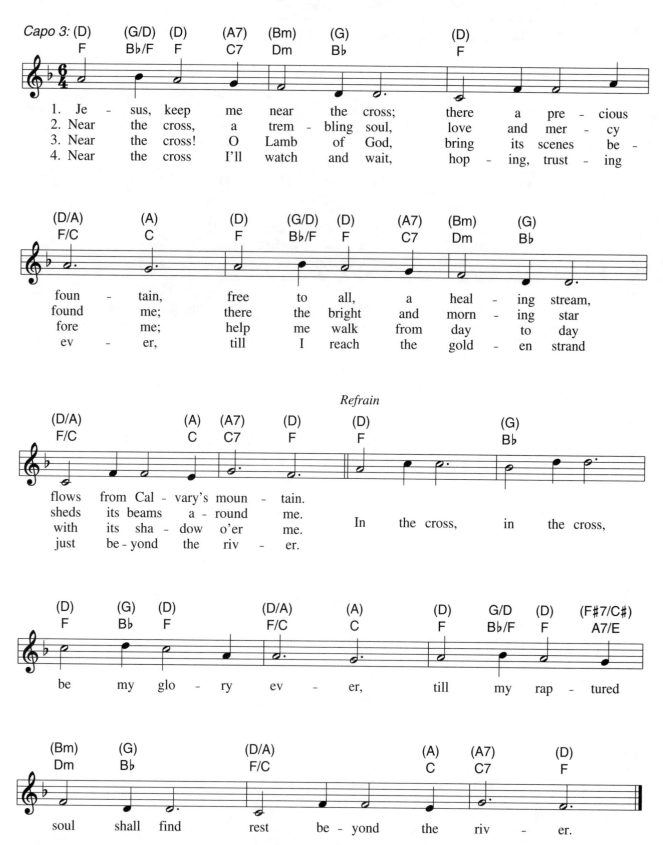

1. Je - sus, keep me near the cross; there a pre - cious
2. Near the cross, a trem - bling soul, love and mer - cy
3. Near the cross! O Lamb of God, bring its scenes be -
4. Near the cross I'll watch and wait, hop - ing, trust - ing

foun - tain, free to all, a heal - ing stream,
found me; there the bright and morn - ing star
fore me; help me walk from day to day
ev - er, till I reach the gold - en strand

Refrain

flows from Cal - vary's moun - tain.
sheds its beams a - round me.
with its sha - dow o'er me.
just be - yond the riv - er.

In the cross, in the cross,

be my glo - ry ev - er, till my rap - tured

soul shall find rest be - yond the riv - er.

WORDS: Fanny J. Crosby
MUSIC: William H. Doane

Christ the Lord Is Risen Today

1. Christ the Lord is risen to - day,
2. Love's re - deem - ing work is done,
3. Lives a - gain our glo - rious King,
4. Soar we now where Christ has led,

Al - le - lu - ia! Earth and heaven in cho - rus say,
Al - le - lu - ia! Fought the fight, the bat - tle won,
Al - le - lu - ia! Where, O death, is now thy sting?
Al - le - lu - ia! Fol - lowing our ex - alt - ed Head,

Al - le - lu - ia! Raise your joys and
Al - le - lu - ia! Death in vain for -
Al - le - lu - ia! Once he died our
Al - le - lu - ia! Made like him, like

tri - umphs high, Al - le - lu - ia! Sing, ye
bids him rise, Al - le - lu - ia! Christ has
souls to save, Al - le - lu - ia! Where's thy
him we rise, Al - le - lu - ia! Ours the

heavens, and earth re - ply, Al - le - lu - ia!
o - pened par - a - dise, Al - le - lu - ia!
vic - tory, boast - ing grave? Al - le - lu - ia!
cross, the grave, the skies, Al - le - lu - ia!

WORDS: Charles Wesley
MUSIC: *Lyra Davidica*, 1708

111 Because He Lives

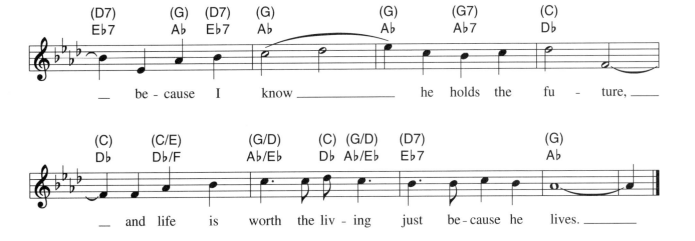

because I know ____ he holds the fu - ture, ____
and life is worth the liv - ing just be - cause he lives. ____

The Strife Is O'er, the Battle Done

112

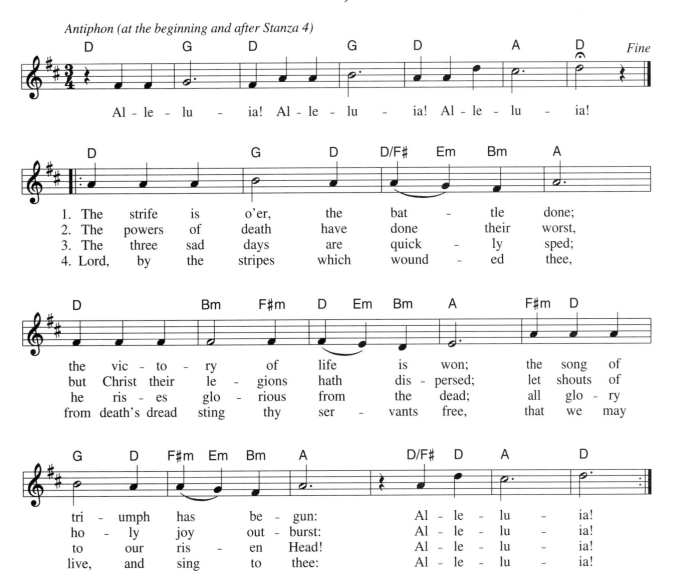

Antiphon (at the beginning and after Stanza 4)

Al - le - lu - ia! Al - le - lu - ia! Al - le - lu - ia!

1. The strife is o'er, the bat - tle done;
2. The powers of death have done their worst,
3. The three sad days are quick - ly sped;
4. Lord, by the stripes which wound - ed thee,

the vic - to - ry of life is won; the song of
but Christ their le - gions hath dis - persed; let shouts of
he ris - es glo - rious from the dead; all glo - ry
from death's dread sting thy ser - vants free, that we may

tri - umph has be - gun: Al - le - lu - ia!
ho - ly joy out - burst: Al - le - lu - ia!
to our ris - en Head! Al - le - lu - ia!
live, and sing to thee: Al - le - lu - ia!

WORDS: Anonymous Latin; trans. Francis Pott
MUSIC: Giovanni P. da Palestrina

113

In the Garden
(I Come to the Garden Alone)

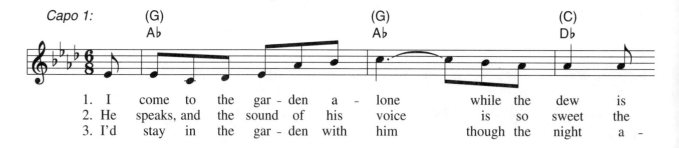

1. I come to the gar-den a-lone while the dew is
2. He speaks, and the sound of his voice is so sweet the
3. I'd stay in the gar-den with him though the night a-

still on the ros-es, and the voice I hear fall-ing on my ear,
birds hush their sing-ing, and the mel-o-dy that he gave to me
round me be fall-ing, but he bids me go; thru the voice of woe

Refrain

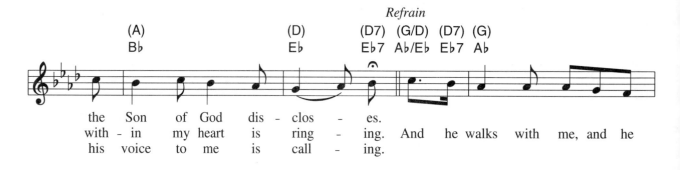

the Son of God dis-clos-es.
with-in my heart is ring-ing. And he walks with me, and he
his voice to me is call-ing.

talks with me, and he tells me I am his own; and the

joy we share as we tar-ry there, none oth-er has ev-er known.

WORDS: C. Austin Miles
MUSIC: C. Austin Miles

Up From the Grave He Arose

1. Low in the grave he lay, Je - sus my Sav - ior,
2. Vain - ly they watch his bed, Je - sus my Sav - ior,
3. Death can - not keep its prey, Je - sus my Sav - ior,

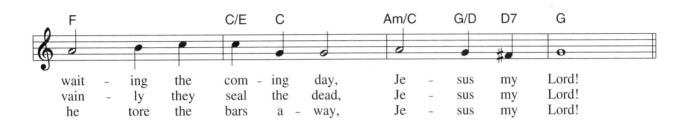

wait - ing the com - ing day, Je - sus my Lord!
vain - ly they seal the dead, Je - sus my Lord!
he tore the bars a - way, Je - sus my Lord!

Refrain

Up from the grave he a - rose, with a might - y tri - umph o'er his

foes; he a - rose a vic - tor from the dark do - main, and he

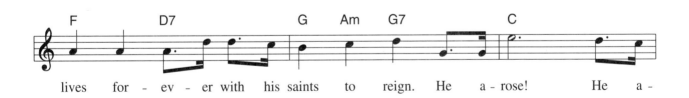

lives for - ev - er with his saints to reign. He a - rose! He a -

rose! Hal - le - lu - jah! Christ a - rose!

WORDS and MUSIC: Robert Lowry

115   Crown Him with Many Crowns

1. Crown him with man-y crowns, the Lamb up-on his throne. Hark! how the heaven-ly an-them drowns all mu-sic but its own. A-wake, my soul, and sing of him who died for thee, and hail him as thy match-less King through all e-ter-ni-ty.

2. Crown him the Lord of life, who tri-umphed o'er the grave, and rose vic-to-rious in the strife for those he came to save. His glo-ries now we sing, who died, and rose on high, who died, e-ter-nal life to bring, and lives that death may die.

3. Crown him the Lord of peace, whose power a scep-ter sways from pole to pole, that wars may cease, and all be prayer and praise. His reign shall know no end, and round his pierc-ed feet fair flowers of par-a-dise ex-tend their fra-grance ev-er sweet.

4. Crown him the Lord of love; be-hold his hands and side, those wounds, yet vis-i-ble a-bove, in beau-ty glo-ri-fied. All hail, Re-deem-er, hail! For thou hast died for me; thy praise and glo-ry shall not fail through-out e-ter-ni-ty.

WORDS: Matthew Bridges and Godfrey Thring
MUSIC: George J. Elvey

Spirit of Faith, Come Down

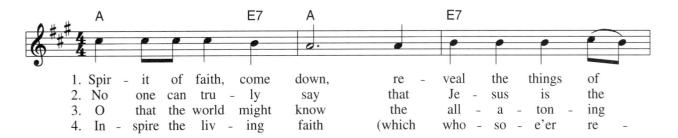

1. Spir - it of faith, come down, re - veal the things of
2. No one can tru - ly say that Je - sus is the
3. O that the world might know the all - a - ton - ing
4. In - spire the liv - ing faith (which who - so - e'er re -

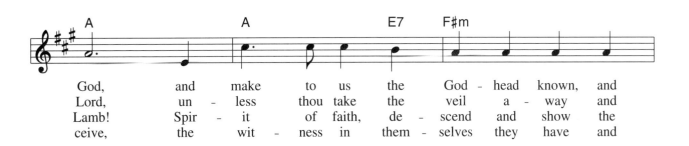

God, and make to us the God - head known, and
Lord, un - less thou take the veil a - way and
Lamb! Spir - it of faith, de - scend and show the
ceive, the wit - ness in them - selves they have and

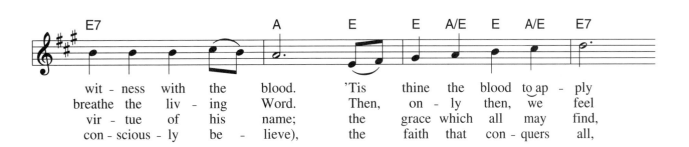

wit - ness with the blood. 'Tis thine the blood to ap - ply
breathe the liv - ing Word. Then, on - ly then, we feel
vir - tue of his name; the grace which all may find,
con - scious - ly be - lieve), the faith that con - quers all,

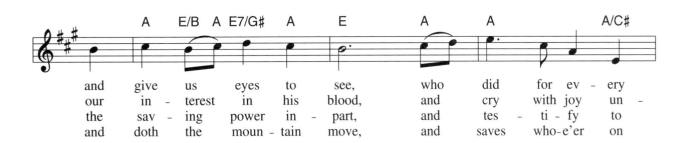

and give us eyes to see, who did for ev - ery
our in - terest in his blood, and cry with joy un -
the sav - ing power in - part, and tes - ti - fy to
and doth the moun - tain move, and saves who - e'er on

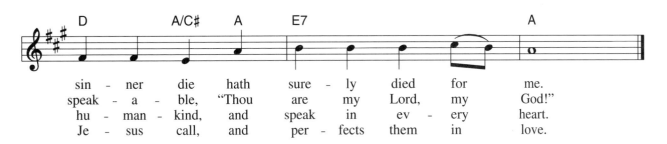

sin - ner die hath sure - ly died for me.
speak - a - ble, "Thou are my Lord, my God!"
hu - man - kind, and speak in ev - ery heart.
Je - sus call, and per - fects them in love.

WORDS: Charles Wesley
MUSIC: *Sacred Harp* (Mason)

117   # Sweet, Sweet Spirit

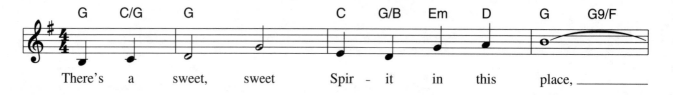

There's a sweet, sweet Spir - it in this place, _____

_ and I know that it's the Spir - it of the

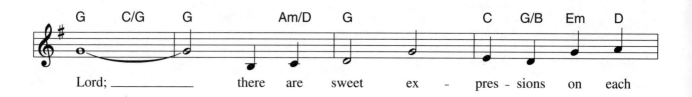

Lord; _____ there are sweet ex - pres - sions on each

face, _____ and I know they feel the pres - ence of the

Refrain

Lord. _____ Sweet Ho - ly Spir - it,

sweet heav - en - ly Dove, stay right here

with us, fill - ing us with your love;

WORDS and MUSIC: Doris Akers
© 1962 Manna Music, Inc.

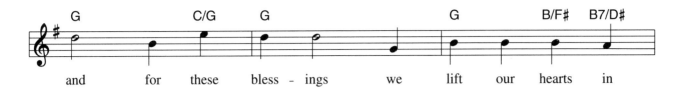

and for these bless - ings we lift our hearts in

praise; with - out a doubt we'll know that we have

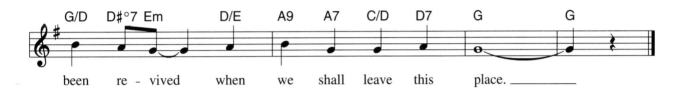

been re - vived when we shall leave this place. _____

Surely the Presence of the Lord 118

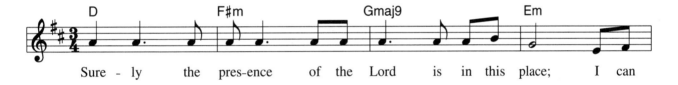

Sure - ly the pres-ence of the Lord is in this place; I can

feel his might - y pow - er and his grace. _____ I can

hear the brush of an - gels' wings, I see glo - ry on each face;

sure - ly the pres - ence of the Lord is in this place.

WORDS and MUSIC: Lanny Wolfe

119   **Only Trust Him**

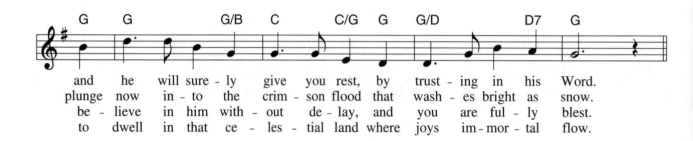

1. Come, ev-ery soul by sin op-pressed, there's mer-cy with the Lord;
2. For Je-sus shed his pre-cious blood rich bless-ings to be-stow;
3. Yes, Je-sus is the truth, the way that leads you in-to rest;
4. Come then and join this ho-ly band, and on to glo-ry go,

and he will sure-ly give you rest, by trust-ing in his Word.
plunge now in-to the crim-son flood that wash-es bright as snow.
be-lieve in him with-out de-lay, and you are ful-ly blest.
to dwell in that ce-les-tial land where joys im-mor-tal flow.

Refrain

On-ly trust him, on-ly trust him, on-ly trust him now.

He will save you, he will save you, he will save you now.

WORDS and MUSIC: John H. Stockton

---

120   **Come, Ye Sinners, Poor and Needy**

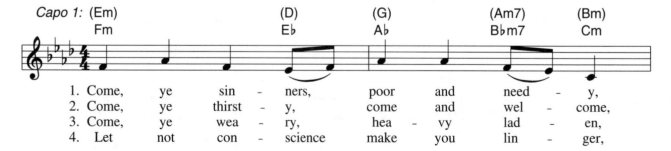

1. Come, ye sin-ners, poor and need-y,
2. Come, ye thirst-y, come and wel-come,
3. Come, ye wea-ry, hea-vy lad-en,
4. Let not con-science make you lin-ger,

WORDS: Joseph Hart
MUSIC: *The Southern Harmony*

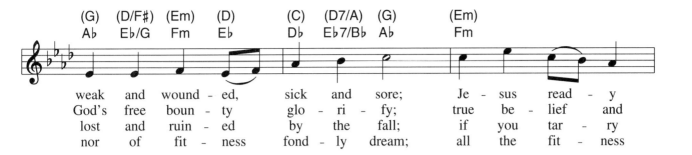

weak and wound - ed, sick and sore; Je - sus read - y
God's free boun - ty glo - ri - fy; true be - lief and
lost and ruin - ed by the fall; if you tar - ry
nor of fit - ness fond - ly dream; all the fit - ness

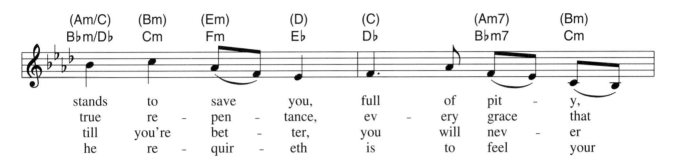

stands to save you, full of pit - y,
true re - pen - tance, ev - ery grace that
till you're bet - ter, you will nev - er
he re - quir - eth is to feel your

Refrain

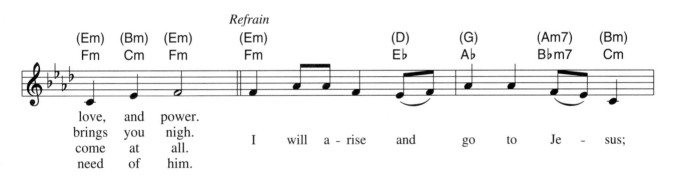

love, and power.
brings you nigh.
come at all. I will a - rise and go to Je - sus;
need of him.

he will em-brace me with his arms; in the arms of

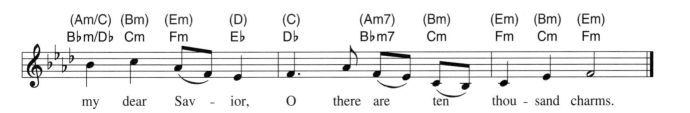

my dear Sav - ior, O there are ten thou - sand charms.

121   Tú Has Venido a la Orilla
(Lord, You Have Come to the Lakeshore)

Tú _____ has ve-ni-do a la o-ri-lla, _____ no has bus-ca-do _____
Lord, _____ you have come to the lake - shore _____ look-ing nei-ther _____

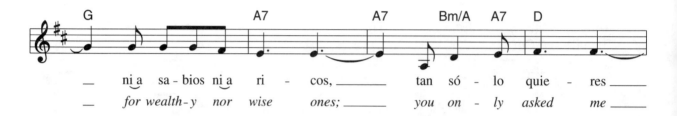

__ ni a sa-bios ni a ri-cos, _____ tan só-lo quie-res _____
__ for wealth-y nor wise ones; _____ you on-ly asked me _____

Estribillo (Refrain)

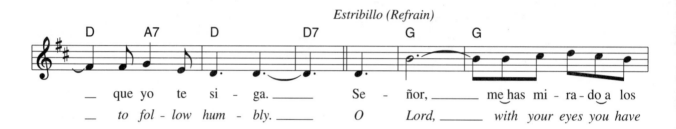

__ que yo te si-ga. _____ Se-ñor, _____ me has mi-ra-do a los
__ to fol-low hum - bly. _____ O Lord, _____ with your eyes you have

o-jos _____ y son-rien-do _____ has di-cho mi nom-bre; _____
searched me, _____ and while smil-ing _____ have spo-ken my name; _____

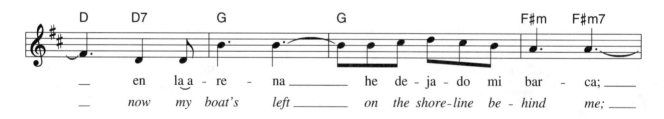

__ en la a-re-na _____ he de-ja-do mi bar-ca; _____
__ now my boat's left _____ on the shore-line be-hind me; _____

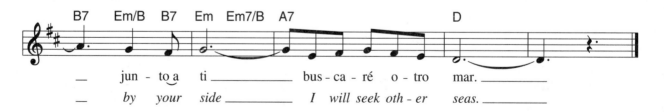

__ jun-to a ti _____ bus-ca-ré o-tro mar. _____
__ by your side _____ I will seek oth-er seas. _____

WORDS: Cesareo Gabaraín; trans. Gertrude C. Suppe, George Lockwood and Raquel Gutiérrez-Achon
MUSIC: Cesareo Gabaraín

'Tis the Old Ship of Zion

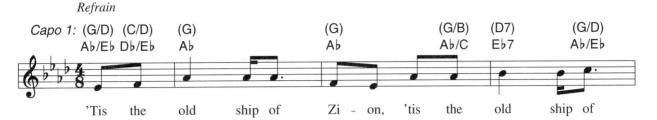

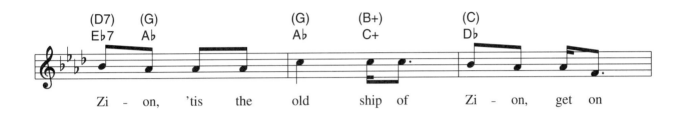

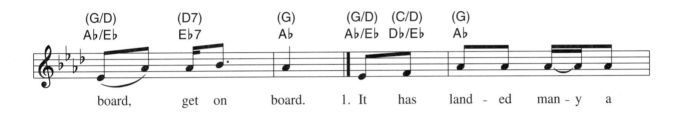

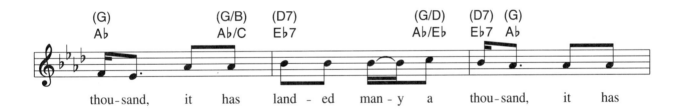

2. Ain't no danger in the water,
3. It was good for my dear mother,
4. It was good for my dear father,
5. It will take us all to heaven,

Other traditional words for the refrain: Give me that
old time religion, . . .it's good enough for me.

WORDS and MUSIC: African American spiritual; adapt. William Farley Smith

123 Spirit Song

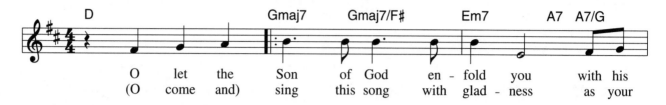

O let the Son of God en-fold you with his
(O come and) sing this song with glad - ness as your

Spir - it and his love. Let him fill your heart and
hearts are filled with joy. Lift your hands in sweet sur -

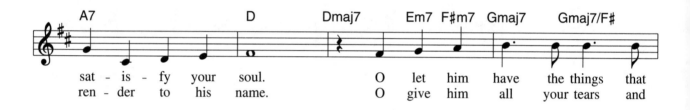

sat - is - fy your soul. O let him have the things that
ren - der to his name. O give him all your tears and

hold you, and his Spir - it like a dove will de -
sad - ness; give him all your years of pain, and you'll

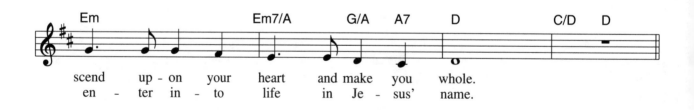

scend up - on your heart and make you whole.
en - ter in - to life in Je - sus' name.

Refrain

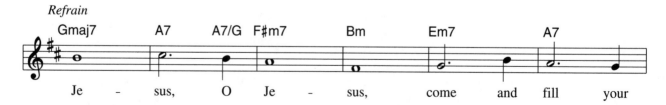

Je - sus, O Je - sus, come and fill your

WORDS and MUSIC: John Wimber

lambs. Je - sus, O Je - sus,

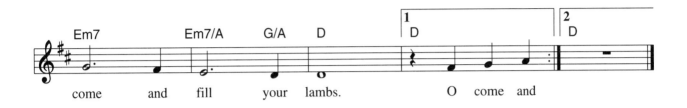

come and fill your lambs. O come and

Turn Your Eyes upon Jesus 124

Turn your eyes up - on Je - sus, look

full in his won - der - ful face, and the

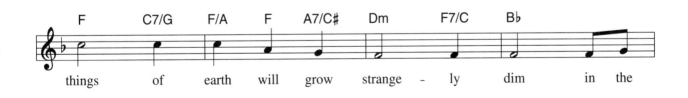

things of earth will grow strange - ly dim in the

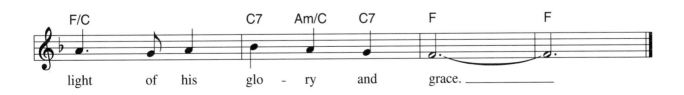

light of his glo - ry and grace.

WORDS and MUSIC: Helen H. Lemmel

125   Softly and Tenderly Jesus Is Calling

WORDS and MUSIC: Will L. Thompson

Pass Me Not, O Gentle Savior

WORDS: Fanny J. Crosby
MUSIC: William H. Doane

127

I Surrender All

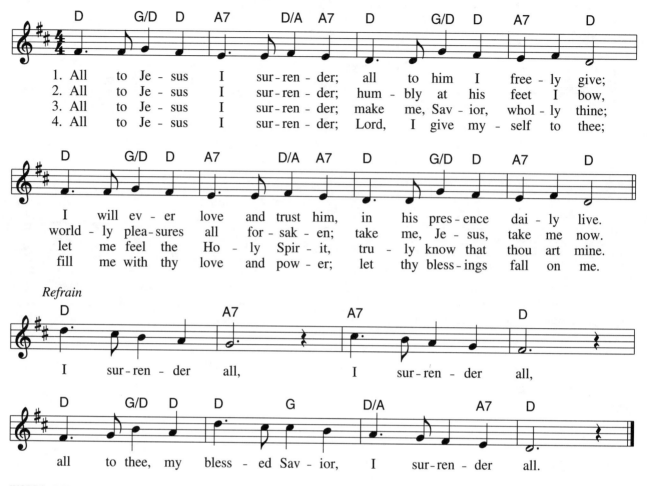

1. All to Jesus I surrender; all to him I freely give;
2. All to Jesus I surrender; humbly at his feet I bow,
3. All to Jesus I surrender; make me, Savior, wholly thine;
4. All to Jesus I surrender; Lord, I give myself to thee;

I will ever love and trust him, in his presence daily live.
worldly pleasures all forsaken; take me, Jesus, take me now.
let me feel the Holy Spirit, truly know that thou art mine.
fill me with thy love and power; let thy blessings fall on me.

Refrain

I surrender all, I surrender all,

all to thee, my blessed Savior, I surrender all.

WORDS: J. W. Van Deventer
MUSIC: W. S. Weeden

128

Just As I Am

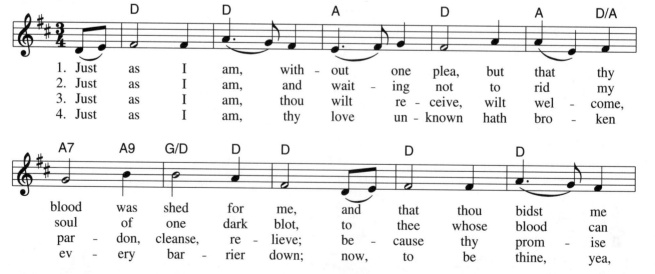

1. Just as I am, without one plea, but that thy
2. Just as I am, and waiting not to rid my
3. Just as I am, thou wilt receive, wilt welcome,
4. Just as I am, thy love unknown hath broken

blood was shed for me, and that thou bidst me
soul of one dark blot, to thee whose blood can
pardon, cleanse, relieve; because thy promise
every barrier down; now, to be thine, yea,

WORDS: Charlotte Elliott
MUSIC: William B. Bradbury

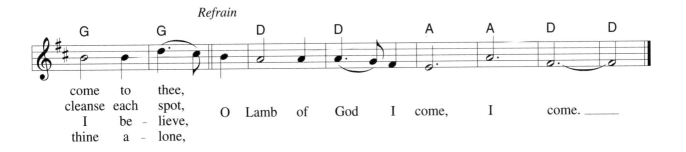

come to thee,
cleanse each spot,
I be - lieve,
thine a - lone,

O Lamb of God I come, I come. _____

Pues Si Vivimos
(When We Are Living)
Shalom to You

129

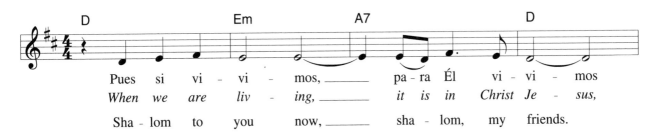

Pues si vi - vi - mos, _____ pa - ra Él vi - vi - mos
When we are liv - ing, _____ it is in Christ Je - sus,
Sha - lom to you now, _____ sha - lom, my friends.

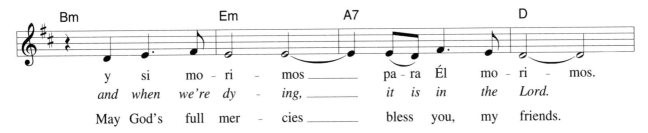

y si mo - ri - mos _____ pa - ra Él mo - ri - mos.
and when we're dy - ing, _____ it is in the Lord.
May God's full mer - cies _____ bless you, my friends.

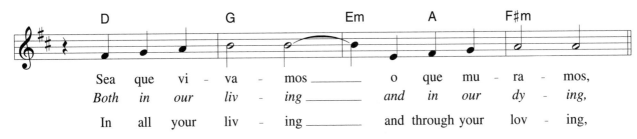

Sea que vi - va - mos _____ o que mu - ra - mos,
Both in our liv - ing _____ and in our dy - ing,
In all your liv - ing _____ and through your lov - ing,

Estribillo (Refrain)   *Repeat Refrain (opt.)*

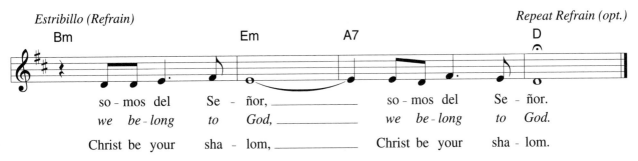

so - mos del Se - ñor, _____ so - mos del Se - ñor.
we be - long to God, _____ we be - long to God.
Christ be your sha - lom, _____ Christ be your sha - lom.

WORDS: St. 1: anonymous; trans. Elise S. Eslinger. St. 2: Elise S. Eslinger
MUSIC: Trad. Spanish melody

St. 1 trans. © 1989 The United Methodist Publishing House; st. 2 © 1983 The United Methodist Publishing House

130

It's Me, It's Me, O Lord
(Standing in the Need of Prayer)

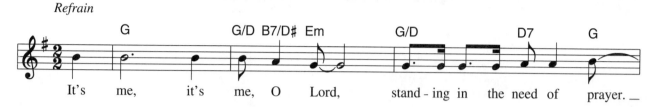

It's me, it's me, O Lord, stand-ing in the need of prayer. —

— It's me, it's me, O Lord, stand-ing in the need of prayer. —

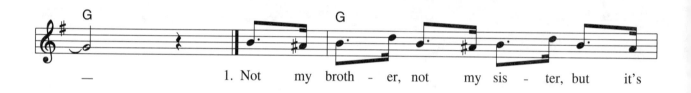

— 1. Not my broth - er, not my sis - ter, but it's

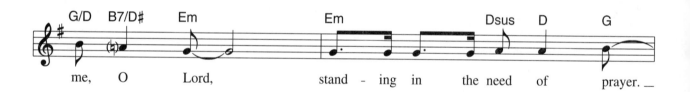

me, O Lord, stand - ing in the need of prayer. —

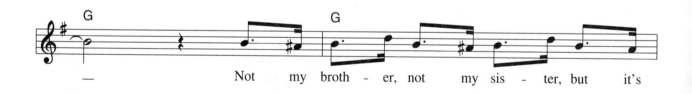

— Not my broth - er, not my sis - ter, but it's

me, O Lord, stand - ing in the need of prayer. —

2. Not the preacher, not the deacon,
3. Not my father, not my mother,

WORDS and MUSIC: African American spiritual

Alas! and Did My Savior Bleed

WORDS: Isaac Watts; refrain by Ralph E. Hudson
MUSIC: Anonymous

132
Rock of Ages, Cleft for Me

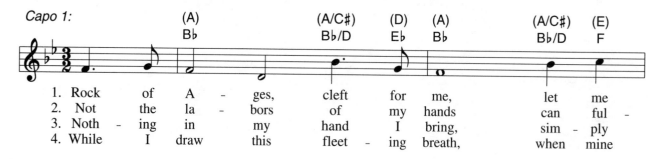

Capo 1:

1. Rock of A - ges, cleft for me, let me
2. Not the la - bors of my hands can ful -
3. Noth - ing in my hand I bring, sim - ply
4. While I draw this fleet - ing breath, when mine

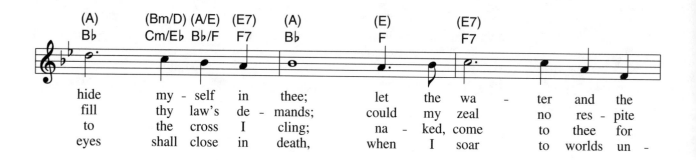

hide my - self in thee; let the wa - ter and the
fill thy law's de - mands; could my zeal no res - pite
to the cross I cling; na - ked, come to thee for
eyes shall close in death, when I soar to worlds un -

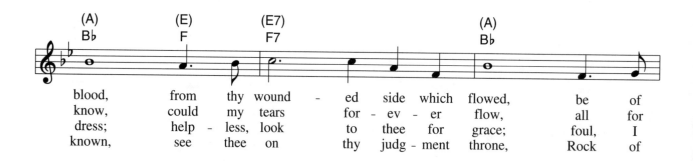

blood, from thy wound - ed side which flowed, be of
know, could my tears for - ev - er flow, all for
dress; help - less, look to thee for grace; foul, I
known, see thee on thy judg - ment throne, Rock of

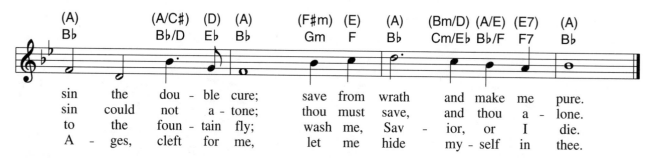

sin the dou - ble cure; save from wrath and make me pure.
sin could not a - tone; thou must save, and thou a - lone.
to the foun - tain fly; wash me, Sav - ior, or I die.
A - ges, cleft for me, let me hide my - self in thee.

WORDS: Augustus M. Toplady
MUSIC: Thomas Hastings

My Hope Is Built

133

1. My hope is built on noth-ing less than Je-sus' blood and
2. When dark-ness veils his love-ly face, I rest on his un -
3. His oath, his cov - e - nant, his blood sup - port me in the
4. When he shall come with trum-pet sound, O may I then in

righ - teous - ness. I dare not trust the sweet-est frame, but
chang-ing grace. In ev - ery high and storm - y gale, my
whelm-ing flood. When all a - round my soul gives way, he
him be found! Dressed in his righ - teous - ness a - lone, fault -

Refrain

whol-ly lean on Je - sus' name.
an-chor holds with - in the veil.
then is all my hope and stay. On Christ the sol - id rock I stand, all
less to stand be - fore the throne!

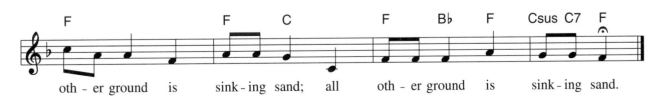

oth - er ground is sink-ing sand; all oth - er ground is sink-ing sand.

WORDS: Edward Mote
MUSIC: William B. Bradbury

134 Grace Greater than Our Sin

1. Mar-vel-ous grace of our lov-ing Lord, grace that ex-
2. Sin and de-spair, like the sea waves cold, threat-en the
3. Dark is the stain that we can-not hide, What can a-
4. Mar-vel-ous, in-fi-nite, match-less grace, free-ly be-

ceeds our sin and our guilt! Yon-der on Cal-va-ry's
soul with in-fi-nite loss; grace that is great-er, yes,
vail to wash it a-way? Look! There is flow-ing a
stowed on all who be-lieve! You that are long-ing to

mount out-poured, there where the blood of the Lamb was
grace un-told, points to the ref-uge, the might-y
crim-son tide, bright-er than snow you may be to-
see his face, will you this mo-ment his grace re-

Refrain

spilt.
cross.
day. Grace, grace, God's grace, grace that will
ceive?

par-don and cleanse with-in; grace, grace, God's

grace, grace that is great-er than all our sin!

WORDS: Julia H. Johnston (Rom. 5:20)
MUSIC: Daniel B. Towner

Nothing but the Blood

135

WORDS and MUSIC: Robert Lowry

136 He Touched Me

WORDS and MUSIC: William J. Gaither

Blessed Assurance

WORDS: Fanny J. Crosby
MUSIC: Phoebe P. Knapp

138   I Stand Amazed in the Presence

1. I stand a - mazed in the pres - ence of
2. For me it was in the gar - den he
3. He took my sins and my sor - rows, he
4. When with the ran - somed in glo - ry his

Je - sus the Naz - a - rene, and won - der how he could
prayed: "Not my will, but thine." He had no tears for his
made them his ver - y own; he bore the bur - den to
face I at last shall see, 'twill be my joy through the

love me, a sin - ner, con - demned, un - clean.
own griefs, but sweat - drops of blood for mine.
Cal - vary, and suf - fered and died a - lone.
a - ges to sing of his love for me.

Refrain

How mar - vel - ous! How won - der - ful! And my

song shall ev - er be: How mar - vel - ous!

How won - der - ful is my Sav - ior's love for me!

WORDS and MUSIC: Charles H. Gabriel (Lk. 22:41-44)

Nothing Between

WORDS and MUSIC: Charles Albert Tindley

140   Standing on the Promises

Capo 3: (G)

1. Stand - ing on the prom - is - es of Christ my King,
2. Stand - ing on the prom - is - es that can - not fail,
3. Stand - ing on the prom - is - es of Christ the Lord,
4. Stand - ing on the prom - is - es I can - not fall,

through e - ter - nal a - ges let his prais - es ring;
when the howl - ing storms of doubt and fear as - sail,
bound to him e - ter - nal - ly by love's strong cord,
lis - tening ev - ery mo - ment to the Spir - it's call,

glo - ry in the high - est, I will shout and sing,
by the liv - ing Word of God I shall pre - vail,
o - ver - com - ing dai - ly with the Spir - it's sword,
rest - ing in my Sav - ior as my all in all,

stand - ing on the prom - is - es of God.
stand - ing on the prom - is - es of God.
stand - ing on the prom - is - es of God.
stand - ing on the prom - is - es of God.

Refrain

Stand - ing, stand - ing, stand - ing on the prom - is - es of

God my Sav - ior; stand - ing,

WORDS and MUSIC: R. Kelso Carter

stand - ing, I'm stand - ing on the prom - is - es of God.

There Is a Balm in Gilead 141

There is a balm in Gil - e - ad to make the wound - ed

whole; there is a balm in Gil - e - ad to

heal the sin - sick soul.

1. Some - times I feel dis -
2. Don't ev - er feel dis -
3. If you can't preach like

cour - aged, and think my work's in vain. But then the Ho - ly
cour - aged, for Je - sus is your friend, and if you look for
Pe - ter, if you can't pray like Paul, just tell the love of

Spir - it re - vives my soul a - gain.
knowl - edge he'll ne'er re - fuse to lend.
Je - sus, and say he died for all.

WORDS and MUSIC: African American spiritual; adapt. William Farley Smith

142   **Amazing Grace**

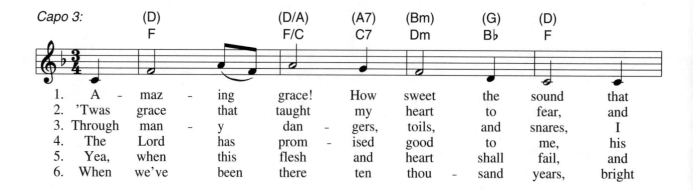

Capo 3:

1. A - maz - ing grace! How sweet the sound that
2. 'Twas grace that taught my heart to fear, and
3. Through man - y dan - gers, toils, and snares, I
4. The Lord has prom - ised good to me, his
5. Yea, when this flesh and heart shall fail, and
6. When we've been there ten thou - sand years, bright

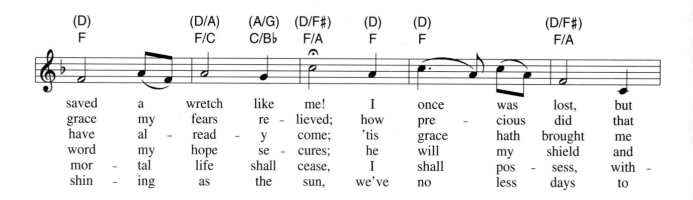

saved a wretch like me! I once was lost, but
grace my fears re - lieved; how pre - cious did that
have al - read - y come; 'tis grace hath brought me
word my hope se - cures; he will my shield and
mor - tal life shall cease, I shall pos - sess, with -
shin - ing as the sun, we've no less days to

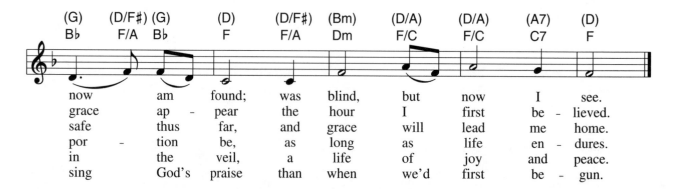

now am found; was blind, but now I see.
grace ap - pear the hour I first be - lieved.
safe thus far, and grace will lead me home.
por - tion be, as long as life en - dures.
in the veil, a life of joy and peace.
sing God's praise than when we'd first be - gun.

WORDS: John Newton; st. 6 anonymous
MUSIC: 19th cent. USA melody

Dona Nobis Pacem

Do - na no - bis pa - cem, pa - cem. Do - na no - bis

pa - cem. Do - na no - bis pa - cem.

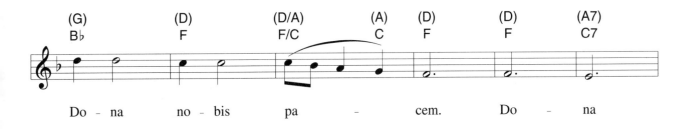

Do - na no - bis pa - cem. Do - na

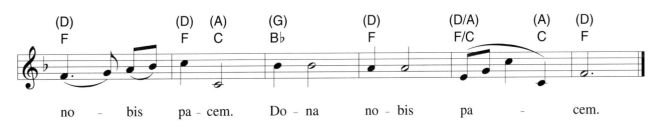

no - bis pa - cem. Do - na no - bis pa - cem.

WORDS: Trad. Latin
MUSIC: Trad.

144 I Cast All My Cares

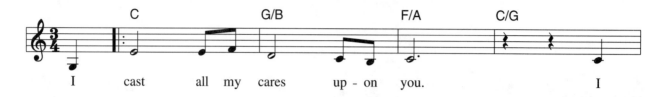

I cast all my cares up-on you. I

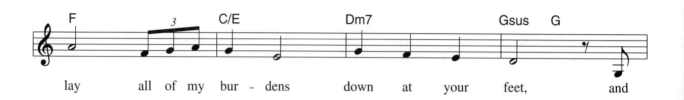

lay all of my bur-dens down at your feet, and

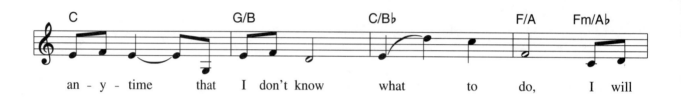

an-y-time that I don't know what to do, I will

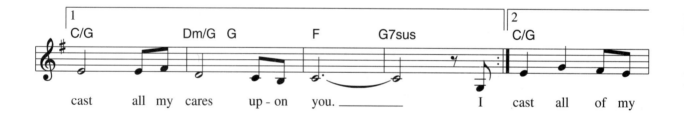

cast all my cares up-on you. _____ I cast all of my

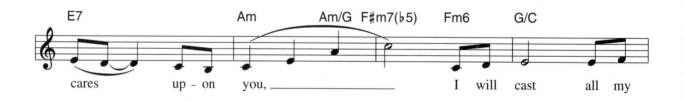

cares up-on you, _____ I will cast all my

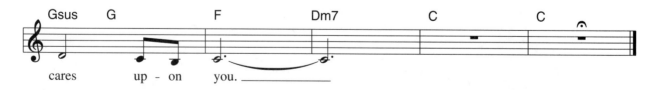

cares up-on you. _____

WORDS and MUSIC: Kelly Willard

Freely, Freely

145

Capo 1:

1. God for-gave my sin in Je-sus' name, I've been born a-gain in Je-sus' name, and in Je-sus' name I come to you, to share his love as he told me to.

2. All power is given in Je-sus' name, in earth and heaven in Je-sus' name, and in Je-sus' name I come to you, to share his power as he told me to.

Refrain

He said, "Free-ly, free-ly you have re-ceived, free-ly, free-ly give. Go in my name, and be-cause you be-lieve, oth-ers will know that I live."

WORDS and MUSIC: Carol Owens
© 1972 Bud John Songs, Inc.

146   Come, O Thou Traveler Unknown

WORDS: Charles Wesley
MUSIC: Trad. Scottish melody

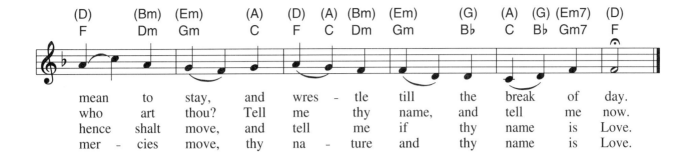

mean to stay, and wres - tle till the break of day.
who art thou? Tell me thy name, and tell me now.
hence shalt move, and tell me if thy name is Love.
mer - cies move, thy na - ture and thy name is Love.

Have Thine Own Way, Lord 147

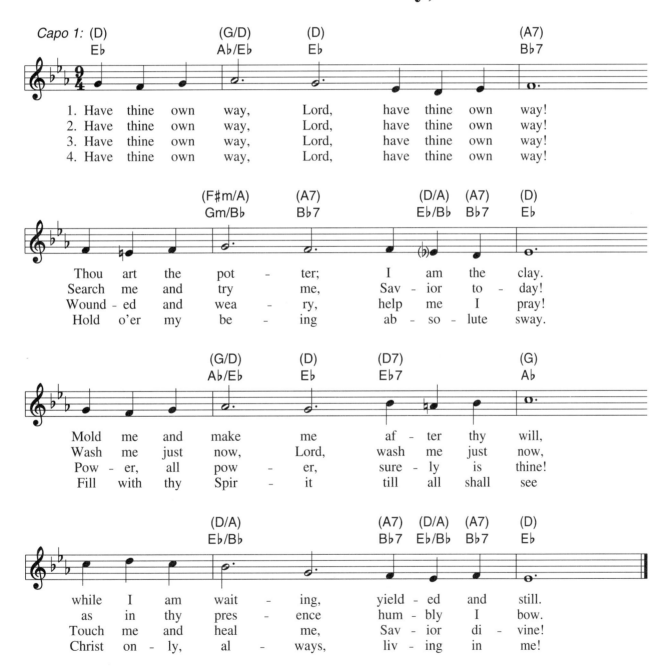

Capo 1: (D)

1. Have thine own way, Lord, have thine own way!
2. Have thine own way, Lord, have thine own way!
3. Have thine own way, Lord, have thine own way!
4. Have thine own way, Lord, have thine own way!

Thou art the pot - ter; I am the clay.
Search me and try me, Sav - ior to - day!
Wound - ed and wea - ry, help me I pray!
Hold o'er my be - ing ab - so - lute sway.

Mold me and make me af - ter thy will,
Wash me just now, Lord, wash me just now,
Pow - er, all pow - er, sure - ly is thine!
Fill with thy Spir - it till all shall see

while I am wait - ing, yield - ed and still.
as in thy pres - ence hum - bly I bow.
Touch me and heal me, Sav - ior di - vine!
Christ on - ly, al - ways, liv - ing in me!

WORDS: Adelaide A. Pollard
MUSIC: George C. Stebbins

148

Spirit of the Living God

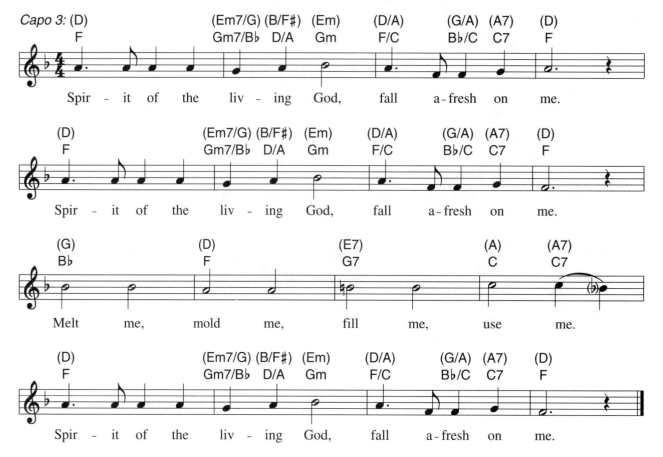

Spir - it of the liv - ing God, fall a-fresh on me.

Spir - it of the liv - ing God, fall a-fresh on me.

Melt me, mold me, fill me, use me.

Spir - it of the liv - ing God, fall a-fresh on me.

WORDS and MUSIC: Daniel Iverson

149

Father, I Adore You

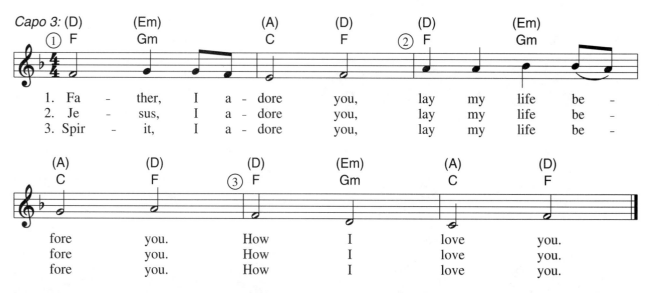

1. Fa - ther, I a - dore you, lay my life be -
2. Je - sus, I a - dore you, lay my life be -
3. Spir - it, I a - dore you, lay my life be -

fore you. How I love you.
fore you. How I love you.
fore you. How I love you.

WORDS and MUSIC: Terrye Coelho (Jn. 13:37; 1 Jn. 3:16)

Change My Heart, O God

150

WORDS and MUSIC: Eddie Espinosa

151 Take Time to Be Holy

Capo 3:

1. Take time to be ho - ly, speak oft with thy Lord;
   a - bide in him al - ways, and feed on his word.
   Make friends with God's chil - dren, help those who are weak,
   for - get - ting in noth - ing his bless - ing to seek.

2. Take time to be ho - ly, the world rush - es on;
   spend much time in se - cret with Je - sus a - lone.
   By look - ing to Je - sus, like him thou shalt be;
   thy friends in thy con - duct his like - ness shall see.

3. Take time to be ho - ly, let him be thy guide,
   and run not be - fore him, what - ev - er be - tide.
   In joy or in sor - row, still fol - low the Lord,
   and, look - ing to Je - sus, still trust in his word.

4. Take time to be ho - ly, be calm in thy soul,
   each thought and each mo - tive be - neath his con - trol.
   Thus led by his Spir - it to foun - tains of love,
   thou soon shalt be fit - ted for ser - vice a - bove.

WORDS: William D. Longstaff
MUSIC: George C. Stebbins

152 I Need Thee Every Hour

Capo 1:

1. I need thee ev - ery hour, most gra - cious Lord;
2. I need thee ev - ery hour; stay thou near - by;
3. I need thee ev - ery hour, most Ho - ly One;

WORDS: Annie S. Hawks
MUSIC: Robert Lowry

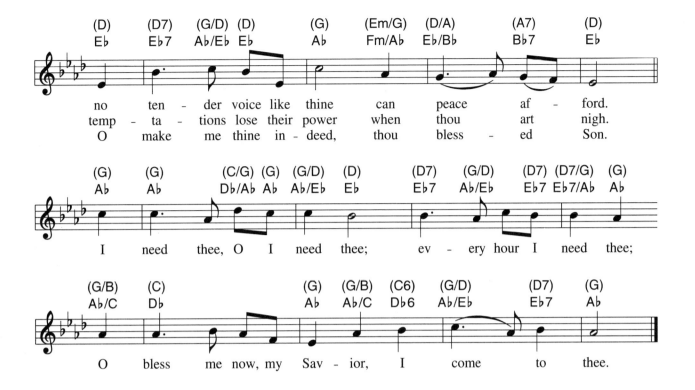

no ten - der voice like thine can peace af - ford.
temp - ta - tions lose their power when thou art nigh.
O make me thine in - deed, thou bless - ed Son.

I need thee, O I need thee; ev - ery hour I need thee;

O bless me now, my Sav - ior, I come to thee.

Jesus Calls Us

153

1. Je - sus calls us o'er the tu - mult of our
2. Je - sus calls us from the wor - ship of the
3. Je - sus calls us! By thy mer - cies, Sav - ior,

life's wild, rest - less sea; day by day his sweet voice
vain world's gold - en store, from each i - dol that would
may we hear thy call, give our hearts to thine o -

sound - eth, say - ing, "Chris - tian, fol - low me!"
keep us, say - ing, "Chris - tian, love me more!"
be - dience, serve and love thee best of all.

WORDS: Cecil Frances Alexander
MUSIC: William H. Jude

154

Take My Life, and Let It Be

1. Take my life, and let it be con-se-cra-ted, Lord, to thee.
2. Take my voice, and let me sing al-ways, on-ly, for my King.
3. Take my will, and make it thine; it shall be no long-er mine.

Take my mo-ments and my days; let them flow in cease-less praise.
Take my lips, and let them be filled with mes-sag-es from thee.
Take my heart, it is thine own; it shall be thy roy-al throne.

Take my hands, and let them move at the im-pulse of thy love.
Take my sil-ver and my gold; not a mite would I with-hold.
Take my love, my Lord, I pour at thy feet its trea-sure-store.

Take my feet, and let them be swift and beau-ti-ful for thee.
Take my in-tel-lect, and use ev-ery power as thou shalt choose.
Take my-self, and I will be ev-er, on-ly, all for thee.

WORDS: Frances R. Havergal
MUSIC: Louis J. F. Hérold

155

Lord, I Want to Be a Christian

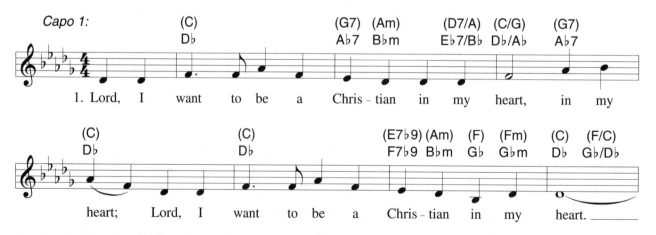

Capo 1:

1. Lord, I want to be a Chris-tian in my heart, in my

heart; Lord, I want to be a Chris-tian in my heart. _____

WORDS and MUSIC: African American spiritual; adapt. William Farley Smith
Adapt. © 1989 The United Methodist Publishing House

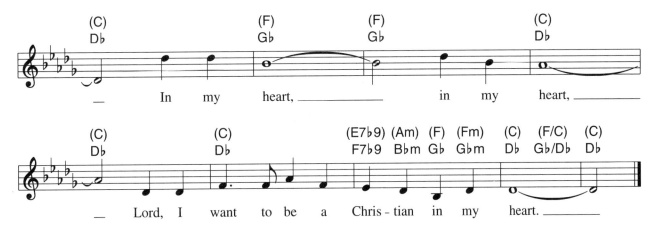

In my heart, _____ in my heart, _____

— Lord, I want to be a Chris-tian in my heart. _____

2. Lord, I want to be more loving in my heart,
3. Lord, I want to be more holy in my heart,
4. Lord, I want to be like Jesus in my heart,

Seek Ye First

156

Al - le - lu - ia,

1. Seek ye first the king - dom of God
2. Ask, and it shall be giv - en un - to you;

al - le - lu - ia,

and his righ - teous - ness, _____
seek, and ye shall find; _____

al - le - lu - ia,

and all these things shall be add - ed un - to you.
knock, and the door shall be o - pened un - to you.

al - le - lu - ia!

Al - le - lu, al - le - lu - ia.
Al - le - lu, al - le - lu - ia.

WORDS and MUSIC: Karen Lafferty

157

Close to Thee

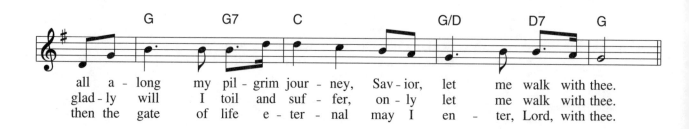

1. Thou my ev - er - last - ing por - tion, more than friend or life to me,
2. Not for ease or world - ly plea - sure, nor for fame my prayer shall be;
3. Lead me through the vale of shad - ows, bear me o'er life's fit - ful sea;

all a - long my pil - grim jour - ney, Sav - ior, let me walk with thee.
glad - ly will I toil and suf - fer, on - ly let me walk with thee.
then the gate of life e - ter - nal may I en - ter, Lord, with thee.

Refrain

Close to thee, close to thee, close to thee, close to thee,

all a - long my pil - grim jour - ney, Sav - ior, let me walk with thee.
glad - ly will I toil and suf - fer, on - ly let me walk with thee.
then the gate of life e - ter - nal may I en - ter, Lord, with thee.

WORDS: Fanny J. Crosby
MUSIC: Silas J. Vail

158

The Gift of Love

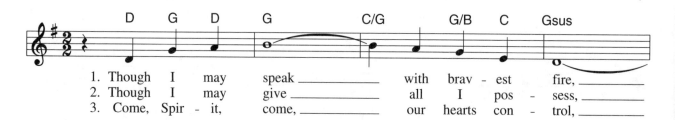

1. Though I may speak _____ with brav - est fire, _____
2. Though I may give _____ all I pos - sess, _____
3. Come, Spir - it, come, _____ our hearts con - trol, _____

WORDS: Hal H. Hopson
MUSIC: Trad. English melody; adapt. Hal H. Hopson
© 1972 Hope Publishing Co.

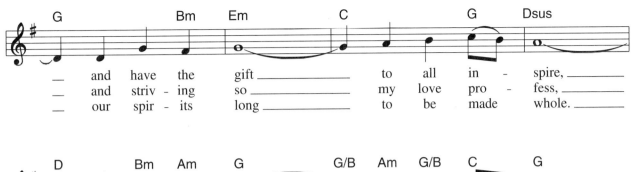

		G			Bm	Em			C						G			Dsus	

_ and have the gift _____ to all in - spire, _____
_ and striv - ing so _____ my love pro - fess, _____
_ our spir - its long _____ to be made whole. _____

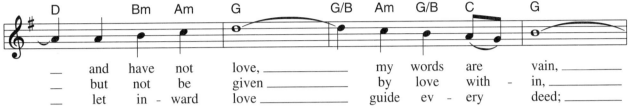

_ and have not love, _____ my words are vain, _____
_ but not be given _____ by love with - in, _____
_ let in - ward love _____ guide ev - ery deed; _____

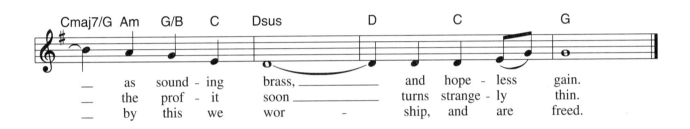

_ as sound - ing brass, _____ and hope - less gain.
_ the prof - it soon _____ turns strange - ly thin.
_ by this we wor - ship, and are freed.

A Charge to Keep I Have

159

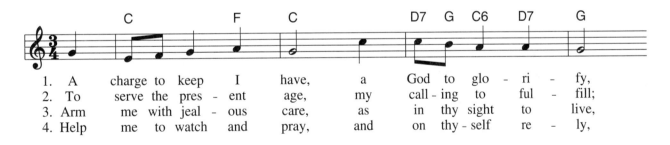

1. A charge to keep I have, a God to glo - ri - fy,
2. To serve the pres - ent age, my call - ing to ful - fill;
3. Arm me with jeal - ous care, as in thy sight to live,
4. Help me to watch and pray, and on thy - self re - ly,

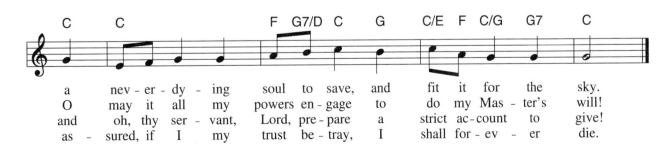

a nev - er - dy - ing soul to save, and fit it for the sky.
O may it all my powers en - gage to do my Mas - ter's will!
and oh, thy ser - vant, Lord, pre - pare a strict ac - count to give!
as - sured, if I my trust be - tray, I shall for - ev - er die.

WORDS: Charles Wesley
MUSIC: Lowell Mason

160   I Want a Principle Within

1. I want a principle within of watch - ful, god - ly fear; a sen - si - bil - i - ty of sin, a pain to feel it near. I want the first ap - proach to feel of pride or wrong de - sire, to catch the wan - dering of my will, and quench the kin - dling fire.

2. From thee that I no more may stray, no more thy good - ness grieve, grant me the fil - ial awe, I pray, the ten - der con - science give. Quick as the ap - ple of an eye, O God, my con - science make; a - wake my soul when sin is nigh, and keep it still a - wake.

3. Al - might - y God of truth and love, to me thy power im - part; the moun - tain from my soul re - move, the hard - ness from my heart. O I want the least o - mis - sion pain my re - a - wak - ened soul, and drive me to that blood a - gain, which makes the wound - ed whole.

WORDS: Charles Wesley
MUSIC: Louis Spohr; adapt. J. Stimpson

Must Jesus Bear the Cross Alone

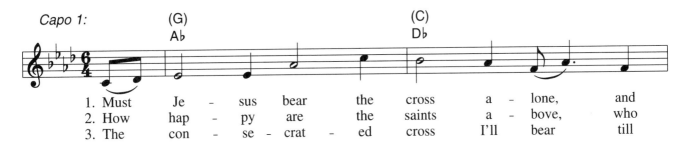

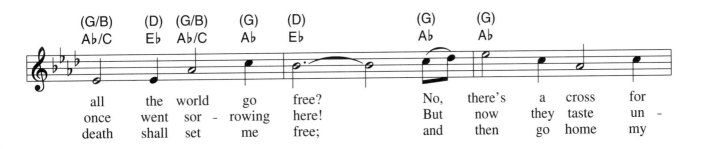

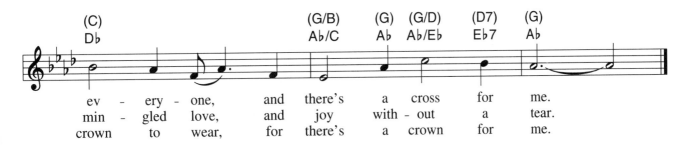

WORDS: Thomas Shepherd and others
MUSIC: George N. Allen

162 I Am Thine, O Lord

WORDS: Fanny J. Crosby
MUSIC: William H. Doane

Humble Thyself in the Sight of the Lord 163

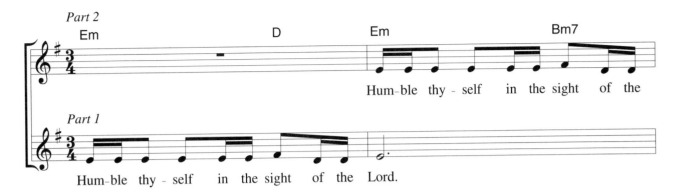

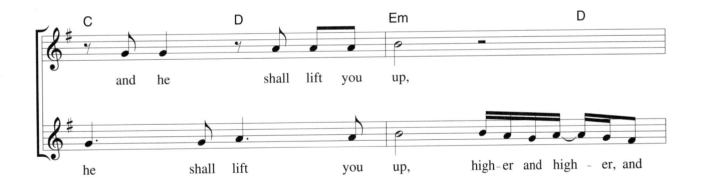

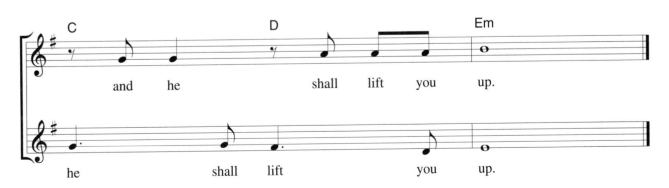

WORDS and MUSIC: Bob Hudson
© 1978, 1983 Maranatha! Music

164   O Master, Let Me Walk with Thee

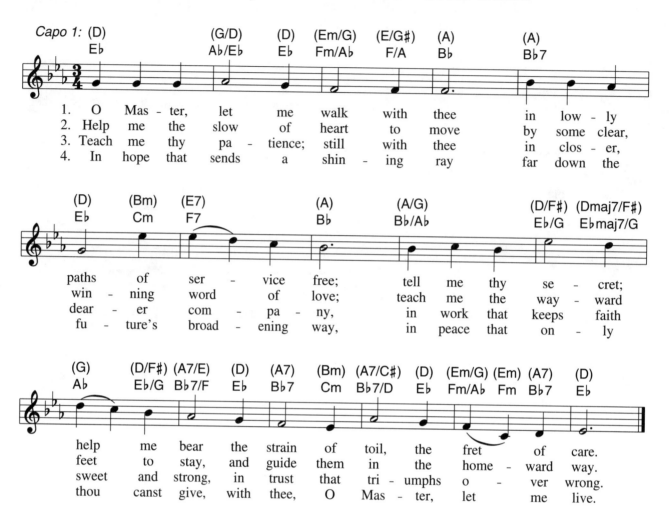

1. O Mas - ter, let me walk with thee in low - ly
2. Help me the slow of heart to move by some clear,
3. Teach me thy pa - tience; still with thee in clos - er,
4. In hope that sends a shin - ing ray far down the

paths of ser - vice free; tell me thy se - cret;
win - ning word of love; teach me the way - ward
dear - er com - pa - ny, in work that keeps faith
fu - ture's broad - ening way, in peace that on - ly

help me bear the strain of toil, the fret of care.
feet to stay, and guide them in the home - ward way.
sweet and strong, in trust that tri - umphs o - ver wrong.
thou canst give, with thee, O Mas - ter, let me live.

WORDS: Washington Gladden
MUSIC: H. Percy Smith

165   Let There Be Peace on Earth

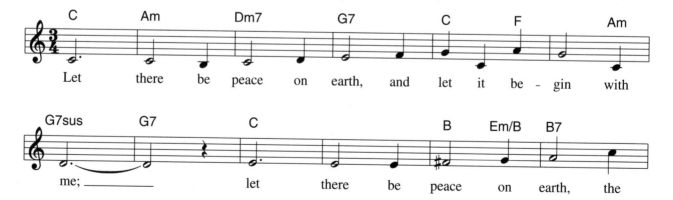

Let there be peace on earth, and let it be - gin with

me; _____ let there be peace on earth, the

WORDS and MUSIC: Sy Miller and Jill Jackson

166   Happy the Home When God Is There

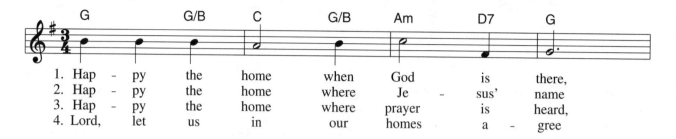

1. Hap - py the home when God is there,
2. Hap - py the home where Je - sus' name
3. Hap - py the home where prayer is heard,
4. Lord, let us in our homes a - gree

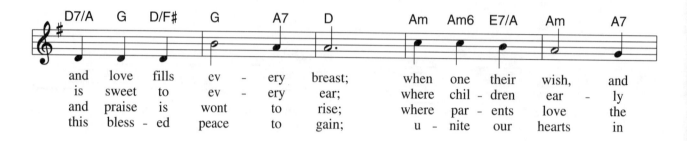

and love fills ev - ery breast;   when one their wish, and
is sweet to ev - ery ear;   where chil - dren ear - ly
and praise is wont to rise;   where par - ents love the
this bless - ed peace to gain;   u - nite our hearts in

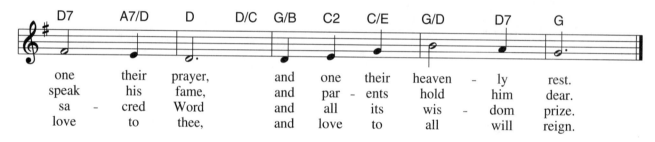

one their prayer, and one their heaven - ly rest.
speak his fame, and par - ents hold him dear.
sa - cred Word and all its wis - dom prize.
love to thee, and love to all will reign.

WORDS: Henry Ware, Jr.
MUSIC: John B. Dykes

167   Jesu, Jesu

Refrain

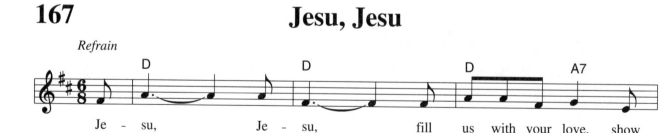

Je - su, Je - su, fill us with your love, show

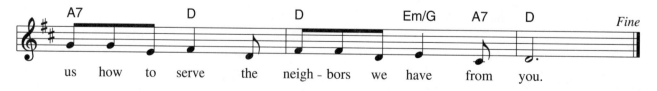

us how to serve the neigh - bors we have from you.

WORDS: Tom Colvin
MUSIC: Ghana folk song; adapt. Tom Colvin

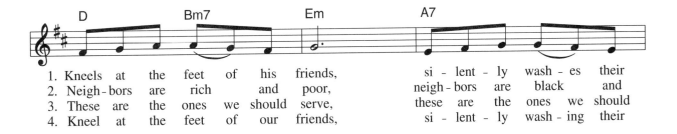

1. Kneels at the feet of his friends, si - lent - ly wash - es their
2. Neigh - bors are rich and poor, neigh - bors are black and
3. These are the ones we should serve, these are the ones we should
4. Kneel at the feet of our friends, si - lent - ly wash - ing their

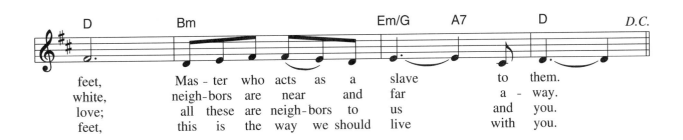

feet, Mas - ter who acts as a slave to them.
white, neigh-bors are near and far a - way.
love; all these are neigh-bors to us and you.
feet, this is the way we should live with you.

Make Me a Servant 168

Make me a ser - vant, hum - ble and meek; Lord, let me

lift up those who are weak; and may the prayer of my

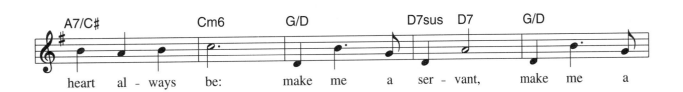

heart al - ways be: make me a ser - vant, make me a

ser - vant, make me a ser - vant to - day.

WORDS and MUSIC: Kelly Willard

169

Cuando El Pobre
(When the Poor Ones)

Dm — A7 — Bb

Cuan-do el po-bre na-da tie-ne y aun re-par-te, _____
When the poor ones who have noth-ing share with strang-ers, _____

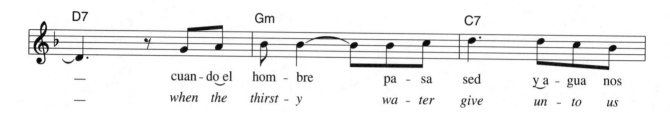

D7 — Gm — C7

— cuan-do el hom-bre pa-sa sed y agua nos
— when the thirst-y wa-ter give un-to us

F — F — E7

da, cuan-do el dé-bil a su her-
all, when the crip-pled in their

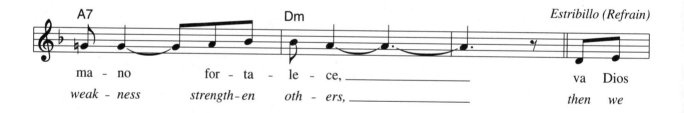

A7 — Dm — *Estribillo (Refrain)*

ma-no for-ta-le-ce, _____ va Dios
weak-ness strength-en oth-ers, _____ then we

Bb — A7 — Dm — D7

mis-mo en nues-tro mis-mo ca-mi-nar, va Dios
know that God still goes that road with us, then we

Gm — A7 — Dm Gm Dm

mis-mo en nues-tro mis-mo ca-mi-nar. _____
know that God still goes that road with us. _____

WORDS: J. A. Olivar and Miguel Manzano; trans. George Lockwood
MUSIC: J. A. Olivar and Miguel Manzano

Please Enter My Heart, Hosanna

170

WORDS and MUSIC: Cathy Townley

171

Be Thou My Vision

Capo 1

1. Be thou my vi - sion, O Lord of my heart;
2. Be thou my wis - dom, and thou my true word;
3. Great God of heav - en, my vic - to - ry won,

naught be all else to me, save that thou art.
I ev - er with thee and thou with me, Lord;
may I reach heav - en's joys, O bright heaven's Sun!

Thou my best thought, by day or by night,
thou and thou on - ly, first in my heart,
Heart of my own heart, what - ev - er be - fall,

wak - ing or sleep - ing, thy pres - ence my light.
great God of heav - en, my trea - sure thou art.
still be my vi - sion, O Ru - ler of all.

WORDS: Ancient Irish; trans. Mary E. Byrne; versed Eleanor H. Hull; alt.
MUSIC: Trad. Irish melody

172

Lord, Have Mercy

Each section is sung first by the Leader and then by All.

Lord, have mer - cy. Christ, have
Ky - ri - e e - le - i - son. Chris - te e -

WORDS: Ancient Greek
MUSIC: James A. Kriewald

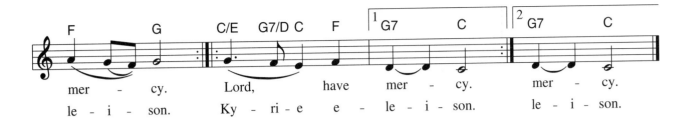

mer - cy.　　Lord,　　have　mer - cy.　　mer - cy.
le - i - son.　Ky - ri - e　e - le - i - son.　le - i - son.

My Faith Looks Up to Thee　　　　173

1. My　　faith　looks　up　to　thee,　　thou　Lamb　of
2. May　　thy　rich　grace　im - part　strength　to　my
3. While　life's　dark　maze　I　tread,　and　griefs　a -
4. When　ends　life's　tran - sient dream,　when　death's　cold

Cal - va - ry,　Sav - ior　di - vine!　Now　hear　me
faint - ing heart,　my　zeal　in - spire!　As　thou　hast
round　me spread,　be　thou　my　guide;　bid　dark - ness
sul - len stream　shall　o'er　me　roll;　blest　Sav - ior,

while　I　pray,　take　all　my　guilt　a - way,
died　for　me,　O　may　my　love　to　thee
turn　to　day,　wipe　sor - row's　tears　a - way,
then　in　love,　fear　and　dis - trust　re - move;

O　let　me　from　this　day　be　whol - ly　thine!
pure,　warm,　and　change - less　be,　a　liv - ing　fire!
nor　let　me　ev - er　stray　from　thee　a - side.
O　bear　me　safe　a - bove,　a　ran - somed　soul!

WORDS: Ray Palmer
MUSIC: Lowell Mason

174 More Love to Thee, O Christ

WORDS: Elizabeth P. Prentiss
MUSIC: William H. Doane

175 Jesus, Remember Me

WORDS: Luke 23:42
MUSIC: Jacques Berthier and the Community of Taizé

Je - sus, re - mem-ber me when you come in - to your king - dom.

Open My Eyes, That I May See

176

Capo 1: (G)

1. O - pen my eyes, that I may see glimps - es of truth thou
2. O - pen my ears, that I may hear voic - es of truth thou
3. O - pen my mouth, and let me bear glad - ly the warm truth

hast for me; place in my hands the won - der - ful key
send - est clear; and while the wave - notes fall on my ear,
ev - ery - where; o - pen my heart, and let me pre - pare

Refrain

that shall un - and set me free. Si - lent - ly now I
ev - ery - thing false will dis - ap - pear.
love with thy chil - dren thus to share.

wait for thee, read - y, my God, thy will to see.

O - pen my eyes, il - lu - mine me, Spir - it di - vine!
O - pen my ears, il - lu - mine me, Spir - it di - vine!
O - pen my heart, il - lu - mine me, Spir - it di - vine!

WORDS and MUSIC: Clara H. Scott

177   # Trust and Obey

1. When we walk with the Lord in the light of his
2. Not a bur-den we bear, not a sor-row we
3. But we nev-er can prove the de-lights of his
4. Then in fel-low-ship sweet we will sit at his

word, what a glo-ry he sheds on our way!
share, but our toil he doth rich-ly re-pay;
love un-til all on the al-tar we lay;
feet, or we'll walk by his side in the way;

While we do his good will, he a-bides with us
not a grief or a loss, not a frown or a
for the fa-vor he shows, for the joy he be-
what he says we will do, where he sends we will

still, and with all who will trust and o-bey.
cross, but is blest if we trust and o-bey.
stows, are for them who will trust and o-bey.
go; nev-er fear, on-ly trust and o-bey.

Refrain

Trust and o-bey, for there's no oth-er way to be

hap-py in Je-sus, but to trust and o-bey.

WORDS: John H. Sammis
MUSIC: Daniel B. Towner

'Tis So Sweet to Trust in Jesus

WORDS: Louisa M. R. Stead
MUSIC: William J. Kirkpatrick

179

I Will Trust in the Lord

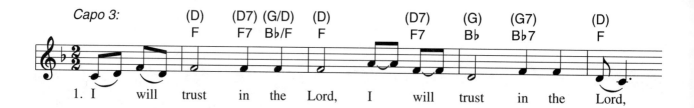

1. I will trust in the Lord, I will trust in the Lord,

I will trust in the Lord, till I die;

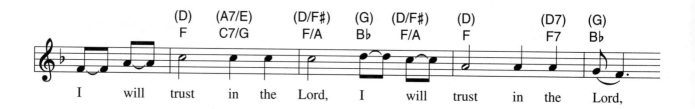

I will trust in the Lord, I will trust in the Lord,

I will trust in the Lord, till I die.

2. Sister, will you trust... till you die?
3. Brother, will you trust...till you die?
4. Preacher, will you trust... till you die?

WORDS and MUSIC: African American spiritual; adapt. William Farley Smith

180

Near to the Heart of God

1. There is a place of qui - et rest, near to the heart of
2. There is a place of com - fort sweet, near to the heart of
3. There is a place of full re - lease, near to the heart of

WORDS and MUSIC: Cleland B. McAfee

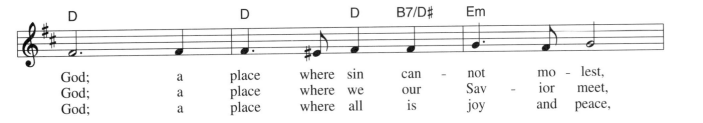

God; a place where sin can - not mo - lest,
God; a place where we our Sav - ior meet,
God; a place where all is joy and peace,

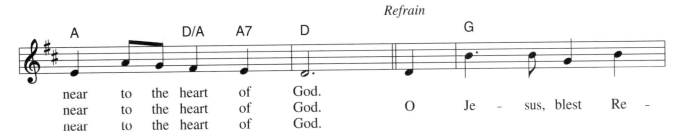

Refrain

near to the heart of God.
near to the heart of God.
near to the heart of God.

O Je - sus, blest Re -

deem - er, sent from the heart of God, hold

us who wait be - fore thee near to the heart of God.

Remember Me

181

Re - mem - ber me, re - mem - ber me,

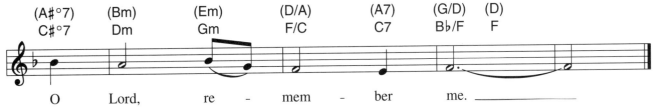

O Lord, re - mem - ber me. _____

WORDS and MUSIC: Trad.

182

Send Me, Lord

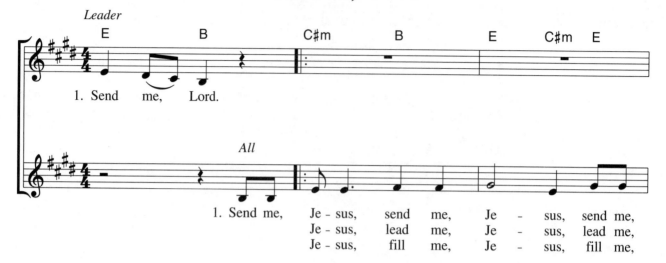

Leader

E   B   C#m   B   E   C#m E

1. Send me, Lord.

All

1. Send me, Je - sus, send me, Je - sus, send me,
Je - sus, lead me, Je - sus, lead me,
Je - sus, fill me, Je - sus, fill me,

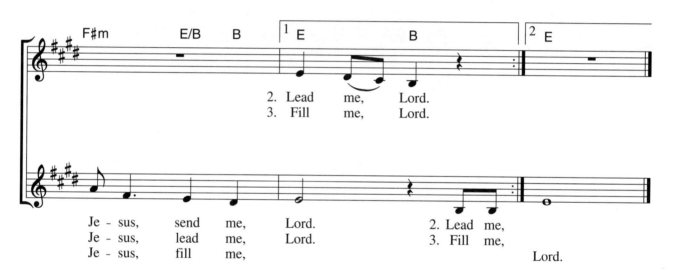

F#m   E/B B |1 E   B |2 E

2. Lead me, Lord.
3. Fill me, Lord.

Je - sus, send me, Lord.   2. Lead me,
Je - sus, lead me, Lord.   3. Fill me,
Je - sus, fill me,   Lord.

WORDS and MUSIC: Trad. South African

183

Lonely the Boat

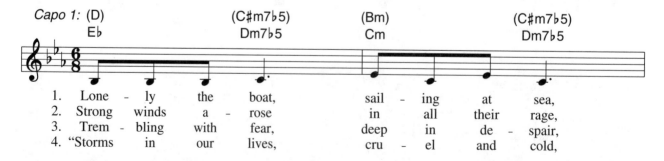

Capo 1: (D)   (C#m7♭5)   (Bm)   (C#m7♭5)
         E♭   Dm7♭5   Cm   Dm7♭5

1. Lone - ly the boat, sail - ing at sea,
2. Strong winds a - rose in all their rage,
3. Trem - bling with fear, deep in de - spair,
4. "Storms in our lives, cru - el and cold,

WORDS: Helen Kim; trans. Hae Jong Kim; versed Hope Omachi-Kawashima
MUSIC: Dong Hoon Lee

184 Sweet Hour of Prayer

1. Sweet hour of prayer! sweet hour of prayer! that calls me from a
2. Sweet hour of prayer! sweet hour of prayer! the joys I feel, the
3. Sweet hour of prayer! sweet hour of prayer! thy wings shall my pe-

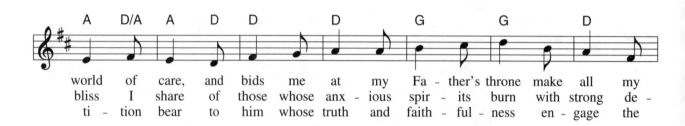

world of care, and bids me at my Fa - ther's throne make all my
bliss I share of those whose anx - ious spir - its burn with strong de-
ti - tion bear to him whose truth and faith - ful - ness en - gage the

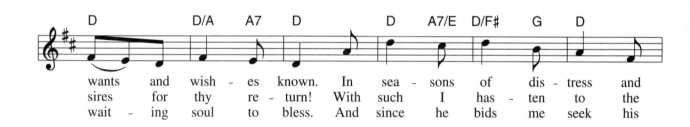

wants and wish - es known. In sea - sons of dis - tress and
sires for thy re - turn! With such I has - ten to the
wait - ing soul to bless. And since he bids me seek his

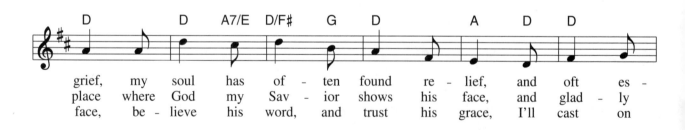

grief, my soul has of - ten found re - lief, and oft es-
place where God my Sav - ior shows his face, and glad - ly
face, be - lieve his word, and trust his grace, I'll cast on

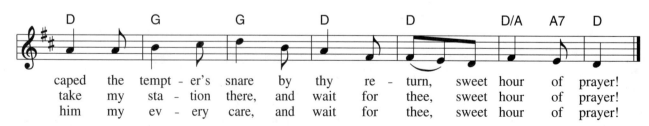

caped the tempt - er's snare by thy re - turn, sweet hour of prayer!
take my sta - tion there, and wait for thee, sweet hour of prayer!
him my ev - ery care, and wait for thee, sweet hour of prayer!

WORDS: William Walford
MUSIC: William B. Bradbury

Kum Ba Yah
(Come By Here)

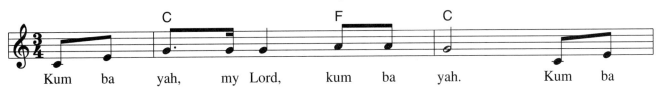

Kum ba yah, my Lord, kum ba yah. Kum ba

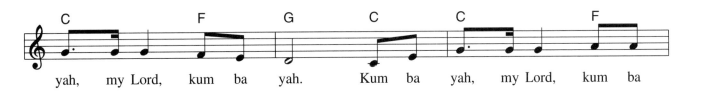

yah, my Lord, kum ba yah. Kum ba yah, my Lord, kum ba

yah. Oh, Lord, kum ba yah!

2. Someone's praying, Lord,...   4. Someone needs you, Lord,...

3. Someone's crying, Lord,...   5. Someone's singing, Lord,...

6. Let us praise the Lord,...

WORDS and MUSIC: African American spiritual

186   Jesus Is All the World to Me

WORDS and MUSIC: Will L. Thompson

Spirit of God, Descend upon My Heart

WORDS: George Croly
MUSIC: Frederick C. Atkinson

188

Thy Holy Wings, O Savior

1. Thy ho-ly wings, O Sav-ior, spread gent-ly o-ver me, and let me rest se-cure-ly through good and ill in thee. O be my strength and por-tion, my rock and hid-ing place, and let my ev-ery mo-ment be lived with-in thy grace.

2. O wash me in the wa-ters of No-ah's cleans-ing flood; give me a will-ing spir-it, a heart both clean and good. And take in-to thy keep-ing thy chil-dren great and small, and while we sweet-ly slum-ber, en-fold us one and all.

WORDS: Caroline V. Sandell-Berg; trans. Gracia Grindal
MUSIC: Swedish folk tune

189

The Old Rugged Cross

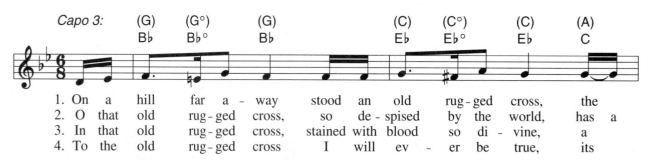

1. On a hill far a-way stood an old rug-ged cross, the
2. O that old rug-ged cross, so de-spised by the world, has a
3. In that old rug-ged cross, stained with blood so di-vine, a
4. To the old rug-ged cross I will ev-er be true, its

WORDS and MUSIC: George Bennard

190

People Need the Lord

With an easy beat (♩ = 92)

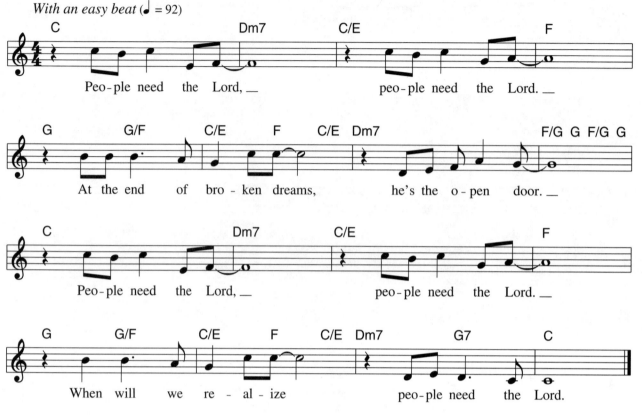

Peo-ple need the Lord, __ peo-ple need the Lord. __

At the end of bro-ken dreams, he's the o-pen door. __

Peo-ple need the Lord, __ peo-ple need the Lord. __

When will we re - al - ize peo-ple need the Lord.

WORDS and MUSIC: Greg Nelson and Phil McHugh

191

There's a Song

Flowing (♩ = ca. 80)

1. There's a song of love in my heart;

love is a gift from Je - sus. There's a song of

love in my heart; love is a gift from God. Al - le -

WORDS and MUSIC: Handt Hanson; adapt. Henry Wiens

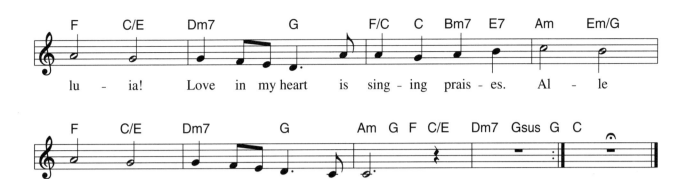

lu - ia! Love in my heart is sing - ing prais - es. Al - le

lu - ia! Love is a gift from God.

2. There's a song of peace in my heart;...
3. There's a song of faith in my heart;...
4. There's a song of hope in my heart;...
5. There's a song of joy in my heart;...

All I Need Is You

192

All I need is you Je - sus, all I need is you.
All I want is you Je - sus, all I want is you.

You are the source of all I need. All I need is
You are the source of all I need. All I want is

you. you. My on - ly hope is you. Lord, my

on - ly hope is you. You are the source of

all I need. My on - ly hope is you.

WORDS and MUSIC: Dan Adler

193 We Shall Overcome

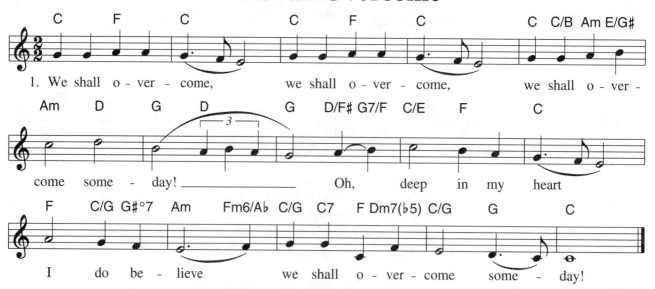

1. We shall o-ver-come, we shall o-ver-come, we shall o-ver-come some-day! _____ Oh, deep in my heart I do be-lieve we shall o-ver-come some-day!

2. We'll walk hand in hand.
3. We shall all be free.
4. We shall live in peace.
5. The Lord will see us through.

WORDS: African American spiritual
MUSIC: African American spiritual

194 Stand by Me

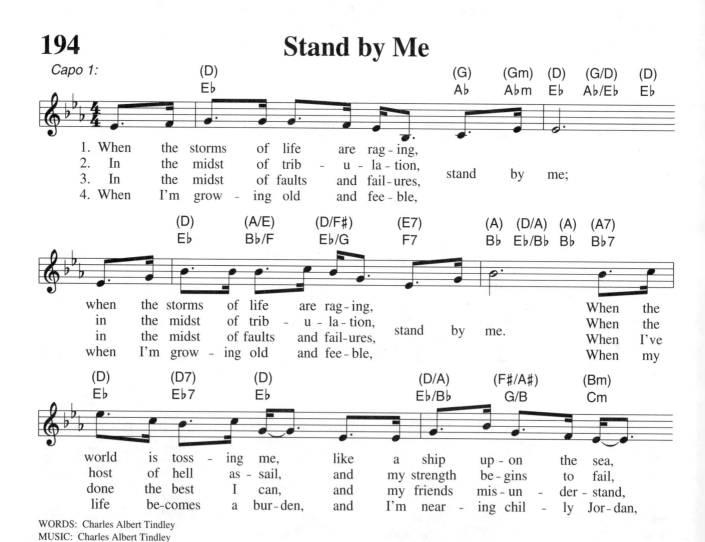

Capo 1:

1. When the storms of life are rag-ing,
2. In the midst of trib - u - la - tion,
3. In the midst of faults and fail-ures,
4. When I'm grow - ing old and fee-ble, stand by me;

when the storms of life are rag-ing,
in the midst of trib - u - la - tion,
in the midst of faults and fail-ures, stand by me.
when I'm grow - ing old and fee-ble,

When the
When the
When I've
When my

world is toss-ing me, like a ship up-on the sea,
host of hell as-sail, and my strength be-gins to fail,
done the best I can, and my friends mis-un - der-stand,
life be-comes a bur-den, and I'm near-ing chil - ly Jor-dan,

WORDS: Charles Albert Tindley
MUSIC: Charles Albert Tindley

thou who rul - est wind and wa - ter,
thou who nev - er lost a bat - tle, stand by me.
thou who know - est all a - bout me,
O thou Lil - y of the Val - ley,

Precious Name 195

Capo 1: (G)

1. Take the name of Je - sus with you, child of sor - row and of
2. Take the name of Je - sus ev - er, as a shield from ev - ery
3. O the pre - cious name of Je - sus! How it thrills our souls with
4. At the name of Je - sus bow - ing, fall - ing pros - trate at his

woe; it will joy and com - fort give you;
snare; if temp - ta - tions round you gath - er,
joy, when his lov - ing arms re - cieve us,
feet, King of kings in heaven we'll crown him,

take it then, wher - e'er you go.
breathe that ho - ly name in prayer. *Refrain* Pre - cious name, O how
and his songs our tongues em - ploy!
when our jour - ney is com - plete.

sweet! Hope of earth and joy of heaven. Pre - cious name,

O how sweet! Hope of earth and joy of heaven.

WORDS: Lydia Baxter
MUSIC: William H. Doane

196

How Firm a Foundation

Capo 1:

1. How firm a foun-da-tion, ye saints of the Lord,
2. "Fear not, I am with thee, O be not dis-mayed,
3. "When through fi-ery tri-als thy path-ways shall lie,
4. "The soul that on Je-sus still leans for re-pose,

is laid for your faith in his ex-cel-lent word!
for I am thy God and will still give thee aid;
my grace, all-suf-fi-cient, shall be thy sup-ply;
I will not, I will not de-sert to its foes;

What more can he say than to you he hath said,
I'll strength-en and help thee, and cause thee to stand
the flame shall not hurt thee; I on-ly de-sign
that soul, though all hell should en-deav-or to shake,

to you who for ref-uge to Je-sus have fled?
up-held by my righ-teous, om-ni-po-tent hand.
thy dross to con-sume, and thy gold to re-fine.
I'll nev-er, no, nev-er, no, nev-er for-sake."

WORDS: "K" in Rippon's *Selection of Hymns*
MUSIC: Early USA melody

197

Nearer, My God, to Thee

1. Near-er, my God to thee, near-er to thee!
2. There let the way ap-pear, steps un-to heaven;
3. Or if, on joy-ful wing cleav-ing the sky,

WORDS: Sarah F. Adams
MUSIC: Lowell Mason

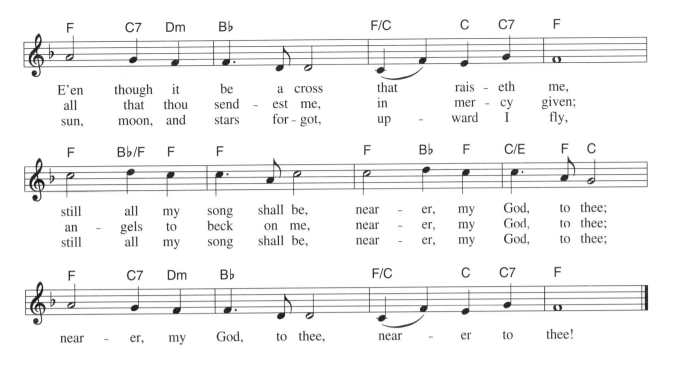

E'en though it be a cross that rais - eth me,
all that thou send - est me, in mer - cy given;
sun, moon, and stars for - got, up - ward I fly,

still all my song shall be, near - er, my God, to thee;
an - gels to beck on me, near - er, my God, to thee;
still all my song shall be, near - er, my God, to thee;

near - er, my God, to thee, near - er to thee!

Come, Ye Disconsolate 198

1. Come, ye dis - con - so - late, wher - e'er ye lan - guish,
2. Joy of the des - o - late light of the stray - ing,
3. Here see the bread of life; see wa - ters flow - ing

come to the mer - cy seat, fer - vent - ly kneel.
hope of the pen - i - tent, fade - less and pure!
forth from the throne of God, pure from a - bove.

Here bring your wound - ed hearts, here tell your an - guish;
Here speaks the Com - fort - er, ten - der - ly say - ing,
Come to the feast of love; come, ev - er - know - ing

earth has no sor - row that heaven can - not heal.
"Earth has no sor - row that heaven can - not cure."
earth has no sor - row but heaven can re - move.

WORDS: Thomas Moore; alt. by Thomas Hastings
MUSIC: Samuel Webbe, Sr.

199   Nobody Knows the Trouble I See

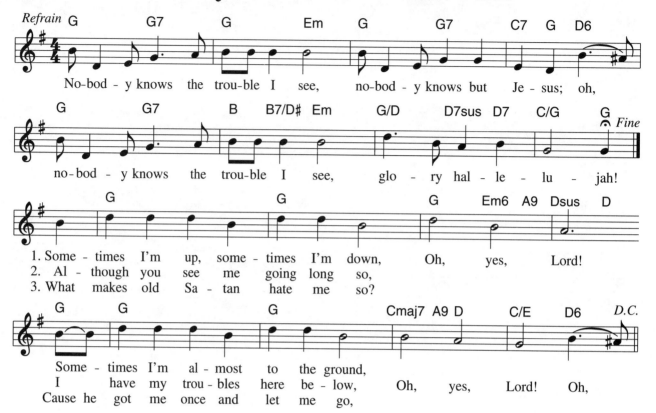

Refrain

No-bod-y knows the trou-ble I see, no-bod-y knows but Je-sus; oh,

no-bod-y knows the trou-ble I see, glo-ry hal-le-lu-jah!

1. Some - times I'm up, some - times I'm down, Oh, yes, Lord!
2. Al - though you see me going long so,
3. What makes old Sa - tan hate me so?

Some - times I'm al - most to the ground, Oh, yes, Lord! Oh,
I have my trou - bles here be - low, Oh, yes, Lord! Oh,
Cause he got me once and let me go,

WORDS: African American spiritual
MUSIC: African American spiritual; adapt. by William Farley Smith
Adapt. © 1989 The United Methodist Publishing House

200   Do, Lord, Remember Me

Capo 3:

1. Do, Lord, do, Lord, do, Lord, re-mem-ber me;

do, Lord, do, Lord, do, Lord, re-mem-ber me;

do, Lord, do, Lord, do, Lord, re-mem-ber me; sing-ing

2. I took Jesus as my Savior, do Lord, remember me.
3. When I'm in trouble, do, Lord, remember me.
4. When I am dying, do, Lord, remember me.
5. I got a home in gloryland that outshines the sun.

WORDS: African American spiritual
MUSIC: African American spiritual; adapt. by William Farley Smith
Adapt. © 1989 The United Methodist Publishing House

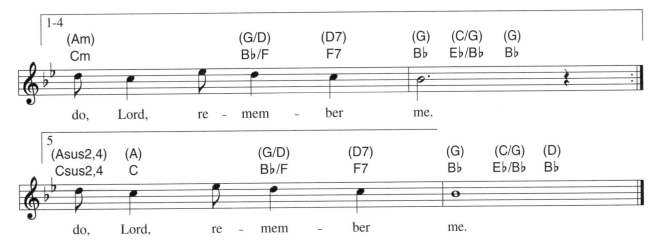

Stand Up, Stand Up for Jesus

201

WORDS: George Duffield, Jr.
MUSIC: George J. Webb

202

Saranam, Saranam
(Refuge)

Refrain

Capo 1:

Je - sus, Sav - ior, Lord, lo, to thee I fly: Sar - a -
nam, Sar - a - nam, Sar - a - nam; thou the Rock, my ref - uge that's
higher than I: Sar - a - nam, Sar - a - nam, Sar - a - nam.

1. In the midst of foes I cry to thee, from the
2. In thy tent give me a dwell - ing place, and be -
3. O that I my vows to thee may pay, and that
4. Yes - ter - day, to - day, for - e'er, the same, lo, the

ends of earth wher - ev - er I may be;
neath thy wings may I find shel - tering grace;
by thy faith - ful - ness to me each day
her - i - tage of all who bear thy name;

my strength in help - less - ness, O an - swer me:
O lift on me the sun - shine of thy face:
may live, and on thy love my bur - dens lay:
to ran - som them from sin the Sav - ior came:

WORDS: Trad. Pakistani; trans. by D. T. Niles
MUSIC: Trad. Punjabi melody

Trans. by permission of Christian Conference of Asia

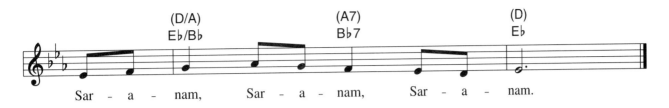

(D/A)   (A7)   (D)
Eb/Bb   Bb7   Eb

Sar - a - nam,   Sar - a - nam,   Sar - a - nam.

Leave It There

203

1. If the world from you with-hold of its sil - ver and its gold, and you
2. If your bod - y suf - fers pain, and your health you can't re-gain, and your
3. When your en - e - mies as - sail, and your heart be - gins to fail, don't for -
4. When your youth - ful days are done, and old age is steal - ing on, and your

have to get a - long with mea - ger fare, just re - mem - ber in his Word how he
soul is al - most sink - ing in de - spair, Je - sus knows the pain you feel, he can
get that God in heav - en an - swers prayer; he will make a way for you, and will
bod - y bends be - neath the weight of care, he will nev - er leave you then, he'll go

feeds the lit - tle bird,
save and he can heal,   take your bur - den to the Lord and leave it
lead you safe - ly through,
with you to the end,

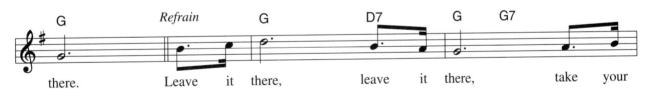

Refrain

there.   Leave it there,   leave it there,   take your

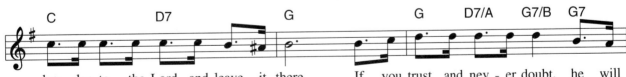

bur - den to the Lord and leave it there.   If you trust and nev - er doubt, he will

sure - ly bring you out; take your bur - den to the Lord and leave it there.

WORDS: Charles Albert Tindley
MUSIC: Charles Albert Tindley
© 1916, renewed 1944 Hope Publishing Co.

204 What a Friend We Have in Jesus

1. What a friend we have in Je - sus,
2. Have we tri - als and temp - ta - tions?
3. Are we weak and heav - y la - den,

all our sins and griefs to bear! What a priv - i - lege to
Is there trou - ble an - y - where? We should nev - er be dis -
cum - bered with a load of care? Pre - cious Sav - ior, still our

car - ry ev - ery - thing to God in prayer!
cour - aged; take it to the Lord in prayer.
ref - uge; take it to the Lord in prayer.

O what peace we of - ten for - feit,
Can we find a friend so faith - ful
Do thy friends de - spise, for - sake thee?

O what need - less pain we bear, all be - cause we do not
who will all our sor - rows share? Je - sus knows our ev - ery
Take it to the Lord in prayer! In his arms he'll take and

car - ry ev - ery - thing to God in prayer.
weak - ness; take it to the Lord in prayer.
shield thee; thou wilt find a sol - ace there.

WORDS: Joseph M. Scriven
MUSIC: Charles C. Converse

Are Ye Able

205

WORDS: Earl Marlatt
MUSIC: Harry S. Mason

206

Pass It On

D   F#m   G

1. It on - ly takes a spark to get a fire
2. What a won - drous time is spring, when all the trees are
3. I wish for you, my friend, this hap - pi - ness that

A6   A   Asus   A   D   F#m

go - ing, _____ and soon all those a - round can
bud - ding; _____ the birds be - gin to sing, the
I've found; _____ you can de - pend on him, it

G   A6   A   Asus   A   G

warm up in its glow - ing. _____ That's how it is with
flow - ers start their bloom - ing. _____ That's how it is with
mat - ters not where you're bound. _____ I'll shout it from the

D/F#   Em7   A7   Dmaj7   Bm7

God's love once you've ex - pe - ri - enced it; you
God's love once you've ex - pe - ri - enced it; you
moun - tain - top; I want my world to know; the

Em7   D/F#   G   A   D

spread his love to ev - ery - one; you want to pass it on. _____
want to sing, it's fresh like spring, you want to pass it on. _____
Lord of love has come to me, I want to pass it on. _____

WORDS and MUSIC: Kurt Kaiser

207

Blest Be the Tie That Binds

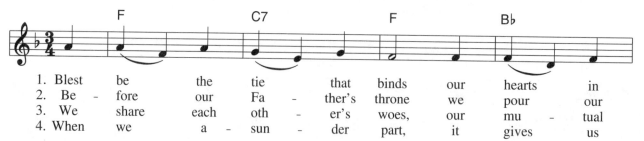

F   C7   F   Bb

1. Blest be the tie that binds our hearts in
2. Be - fore our Fa - ther's throne we pour our
3. We share each oth - er's woes, our mu - tual
4. When we a - sun - der part, it gives us

WORDS: John Fawcett
MUSIC: Johann G. Nägeli

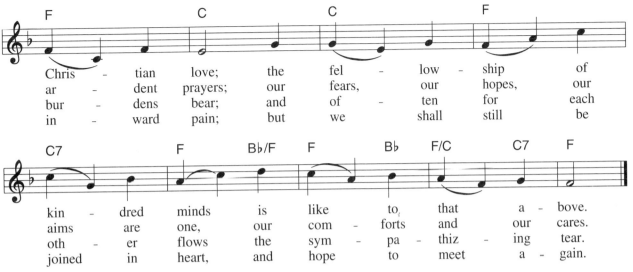

F		C		C		F	
Chris	tian	love;	the	fel	low	ship	of
ar	dent	prayers;	our	fears,	our	hopes,	our
bur	dens	bear;	and	of	ten	for	each
in	ward	pain;	but	we	shall	still	be

C7		F	Bb/F	F	Bb	F/C	C7	F
kin	dred	minds	is	like	to	that	a	bove.
aims	are	one,	our	com	forts	and	our	cares.
oth	er	flows	the	sym	pa	thiz	ing	tear.
joined	in	heart,	and	hope	to	meet	a	gain.

We Are the Church

208

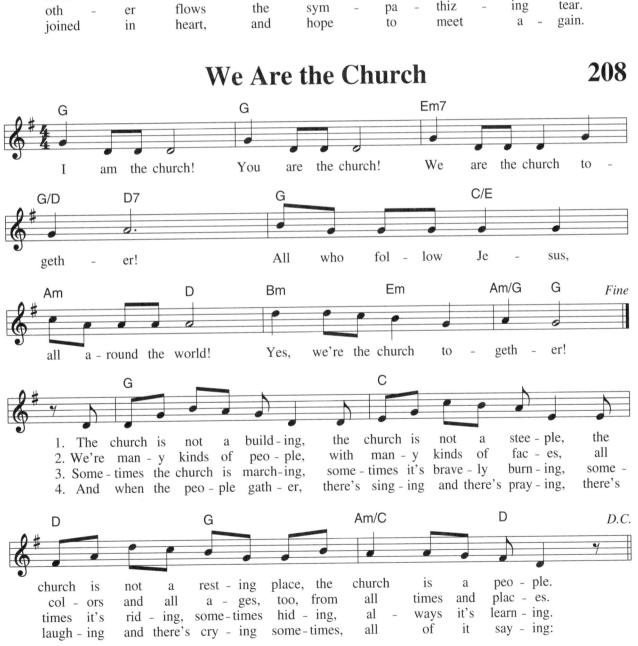

G			G			Em7	
I	am	the church!	You	are	the church!	We	are the church to-

G/D	D7		G		C/E	
geth	er!		All	who	fol low	Je - sus,

Am		D		Bm		Em		Am/G	G	*Fine*
all	a - round the world!	Yes,	we're the church	to - geth - er!						

G		C	
1. The church is not a build-ing,	the church is not a stee-ple,	the
2. We're man - y kinds of peo-ple,	with man - y kinds of fac - es,	all
3. Some-times the church is march-ing,	some-times it's brave-ly burn-ing,	some-
4. And when the peo - ple gath - er,	there's sing-ing and there's pray-ing,	there's

D		G		Am/C		D		*D.C.*
church is not a rest - ing place, the	church is a peo - ple.							
col - ors and all a - ges, too, from	all times and plac - es.							
times it's rid - ing, some-times hid - ing,	al - ways it's learn - ing.							
laugh - ing and there's cry - ing some-times,	all of it say - ing:							

WORDS and MUSIC: Richard K. Avery and Donald S. Marsh

© 1972 Hope Publishing Co.

209

Sois la Semilla
(You Are the Seed)

Sois la se- mi- lla que ha de cre- cer, sois es-
Sois la ma- ña- na que vuel- ve a na- cer, sois es-

You are the seed that will grow a new sprout; you're a
You are the dawn that will bring a new day; you're the

tre- lla que ha de bri- llar. Sois le- va- du- ra, sois
pi- ga que em- pie- za a gra- nar. Sois a gui- jón y ca-

star that will shine in the night; you are the yeast and a
wheat that will bear gold- en grain; you are a sting and a

gra- no de sal, an- tor- cha que de- be a- lum- brar.
ri- cía a la vez, tes- ti- gos que voy a en- viar.

small grain of salt, a bea- con to glow in the dark.
soft, gen- tle touch, my wit- ness- es wher- e'er you go.

Refrain

Id, a- mi- gos, por el mun- do, a- nun- cian- do el a-
Sed, a- mi- gos, mis tes- ti- gos de mi re- su- rrec-

Go, my friends, go to the world, pro- claim- ing love to
Be, my friends, a loy- al wit- ness, from the dead I a-

mor, men- sa- je- ros de la vi- da,
ción. Id lle- van- do mi pre- sen- cia;

all, mes- sen- gers of my for- giv- ing peace,
rose; "Lo, I'll be with you for- ev- er,

1. de la paz y el per- dón.
e- ter- nal love.

2. con vo- so- tros es- toy.
till the end of the world."

WORDS: Cesareo Gabaraín; trans. by Raquel Guitérrez-Achon and Skinner Chávez-Melo
MUSIC: Cesareo Gabaraín

The Church's One Foundation

1. The church-'s one foun - da - tion is Je - sus Christ her Lord; she is his new cre - a - tion by wa - ter and the Word. From heaven he came and sought her to be his ho - ly bride; with his own blood he bought her, and for her life he died.

2. E - lect from ev - ery na - tion, yet one o'er all the earth; her char - ter of sal - va - tion, one Lord, one faith, one birth; one ho - ly name she bless - es, par - takes one ho - ly food, and to one hope she press - es, with ev - ery grace en - dued.

3. Mid toil and trib - u - la - tion, and tu - mult of her war, she waits the con - sum - ma - tion of peace for - ev - er - more; till, with the vi - sion glo - rious, her long - ing eyes are blest, and the great church vic - to - rious shall be the church at rest.

4. Yet she on earth hath un - ion with God the Three in One, and mys - tic sweet com - mu - nion with those whose rest is won. O hap - py ones and ho - ly! Lord, give us grace that we like them, the meek and low - ly, on high may dwell with thee.

WORDS: Samuel J. Stone
MUSIC: Samuel Sebastian Wesley

211 **Onward Christian Soldiers**

1. On-ward, Chris-tian sol - diers, march-ing as to war, with the cross of Je - sus go-ing on be - fore.
2. Like a might-y ar - my moves the church of God; broth-ers, we are tread - ing where the saints have trod.
3. On-ward then, ye peo - ple, join our hap-py throng, blend with ours your voic - es in the tri - umph song.

Christ, the roy - al Mas - ter, leads a - gainst the foe; for - ward in - to bat - tle see his ban - ners go!
We are not di - vid - ed, all one bod - y we, one in hope and doc - trine, one in char - i - ty.
Glo - ry, laud, and hon - or un - to Christ the King, this through count-less a - ges men and an - gels sing.

Refrain

On - ward, Chris-tian sol - diers, march-ing as to war,

WORDS: Sabine Baring-Gould
MUSIC: Arthur S. Sullivan

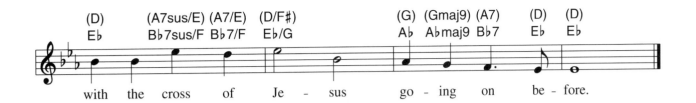

with the cross of Je - sus go - ing on be - fore.

They'll Know We Are Christians
by Our Love

212

Capo 1:

1. We are one in the Spir - it, we are one in the Lord.
2. We will walk with each oth - er, we will walk hand in hand.
3. We will work with each oth - er, we will work side by side.
4. All praise to the Fa - ther, from whom all things come,

We are one in the Spir - it, we are one in the Lord,
We will walk with each oth - er, we will walk hand in hand,
We will work with each oth - er, we will work side by side,
and all praise to Christ Je - sus, his on - ly Son,

and we pray that all u - ni - ty may one day be re - stored:
and to - geth - er we'll spread the news that God is in our land:
and we'll guard each one's dig - ni - ty and save hu - man pride:
and all praise to the Spir - it who makes us one:

And they'll know we are Chris - tians by our love, by our love.

Yes, they'll know we are Chris - tians by our love. _____

WORDS and MUSIC: Peter Scholtes

213

Here I Am, Lord

1. I, the Lord of sea and sky, / I have heard my
I who made the stars of night, / I will make their

2. I, the Lord of snow and rain, / I have borne my
I will break their hearts of stone, / give them hearts for

3. I, the Lord of wind and flame, / I will tend the
Fin-est bread I will pro-vide / till their hearts be

peo-ple cry. All who dwell in dark and sin
dark-ness bright. Who will bear my light to them?

peo-ple's pain. I have wept for love of them.
love a-lone. I will speak my word to them.

poor and lame, I will set a feast for them.
sat-is-fied. I will give my life to them.

1. my hand will save.
They turn a-way.
My hand will save.

2. Whom shall I send? _____
Whom shall I send? _____
Whom shall I send? _____

Refrain

Here I am, Lord. ____ Is it I, Lord? ____ I have heard you
call-ing in the night. _____ I will go, Lord, _____ if you
lead me. _____ I will hold your peo-ple in my heart.

WORDS: Dan Schutte
MUSIC: Dan Schutte; adapt. by Carlton R. Young
© 1981, 1983, 1989 Daniel L. Schutte and NALR

Wonderful Words of Life

1. Sing them o - ver a - gain to me, won-der-ful words of life;
2. Christ, the bless-ed one, gives to all won-der-ful words of life;
3. Sweet - ly ech - o the gos - pel call, won-der-ful words of life;

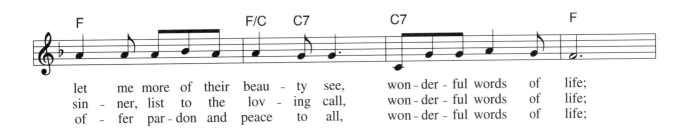

let me more of their beau - ty see, won-der-ful words of life;
sin - ner, list to the lov - ing call, won-der-ful words of life;
of - fer par-don and peace to all, won-der-ful words of life;

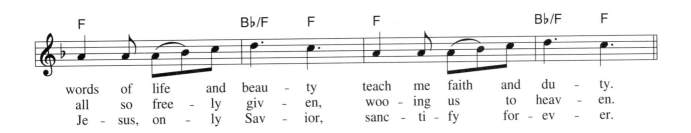

words of life and beau - ty teach me faith and du - ty.
all so free - ly giv - en, woo - ing us to heav - en.
Je - sus, on - ly Sav - ior, sanc - ti - fy for - ev - er.

Refrain

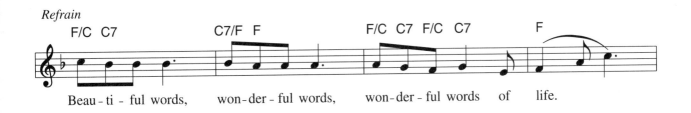

Beau-ti-ful words, won-der-ful words, won-der-ful words of life.

Beau-ti-ful words, won-der-ful words, won-der-ful words of life.

WORDS and MUSIC: Philip P. Bliss

215 Break Thou the Bread of Life

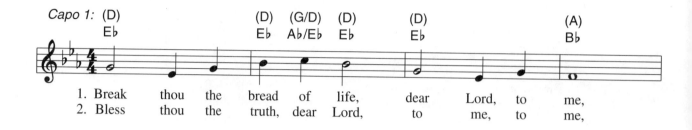

1. Break thou the bread of life, dear Lord, to me,
2. Bless thou the truth, dear Lord, to me, to me,

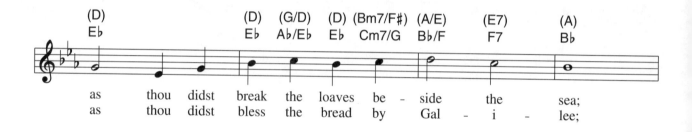

as thou didst break the loaves be - side the sea;
as thou didst bless the bread by Gal - i - lee;

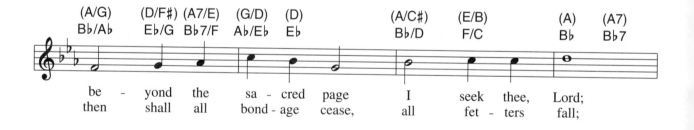

be - yond the sa - cred page I seek thee, Lord;
then shall all bond - age cease, all fet - ters fall;

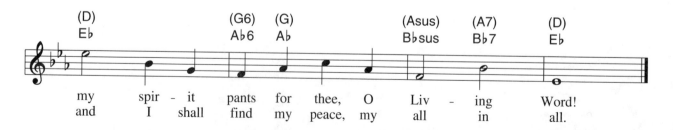

my spir - it pants for thee, O Liv - ing Word!
and I shall find my peace, my all in all.

WORDS: Mary A. Lathbury
MUSIC: William F. Sherwin

Holy Ground

We are stand - ing _____ on ho - ly ground, _____ and I

know that there are an - gels all a - round. _____ Let us

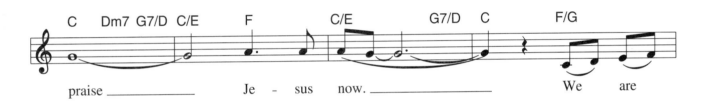

praise _____ Je - sus now. _____ We are

stand - ing in his pres - ence on ho - ly ground. _____

WORDS and MUSIC: Geron Davis

© 1983 Meadowgreen Music Co./Songchannel Music Co. (MG)

217

Let Us Break Bread Together

1. Let us break bread to-geth-er on our knees,
2. Let us drink wine to-geth-er on our knees,
3. Let us praise God to-geth-er on our knees,

— let us break bread to-geth-er on our
— let us drink wine to-geth-er on our
— let us praise God to-geth-er on our

knees.
knees.
knees.

When I fall on my

knees with my face to the ris-ing sun, O

Lord, have mer-cy on me.

WORDS: African American spiritual
MUSIC: African American spiritual; adapt. by William Farley Smith

Adapt. © 1989 The United Methodist Publishing House

218

Eat This Bread

Eat this bread, drink this cup, come to me and nev-er be hun-gry.

WORDS: Robert Batastini and the Taizé Community
MUSIC: Jacques Berthier

© 1984 Les Presses de Taizé France; by permission of G.I.A. Publications, Inc.

Eat this bread, drink this cup, trust in me and you will not thirst.

Come, Let Us Eat

219

Leader

Capo 3: (D) / F

1. Come, let us eat, for now the feast is spread._____
2. Come let us drink, for now the wine is poured._____
3. In his pres - ence now we meet and rest,_____
4. Rise, then, to spread a - broad God's might - y Word._____

All

Come, let us eat, for now the feast is spread._____
Come let us drink, for now the wine is poured._____
In his pres - ence now we meet and rest,_____
Rise, then, to spread a - broad God's might - y Word._____

Leader

Our Lord's bod - y let us take to - geth - er._____
Je - sus' blood poured let us drink to - geth - er._____
In the pres - ence of our Lord we gath - er._____
Je - sus ris - en will bring in the king - dom._____

All

Our Lord's bod - y let us take to - geth - er._____
Je - sus' blood poured let us drink to - geth - er._____
In the pres - ence of our Lord we gath - er._____
Je - sus ris - en will bring in the king - dom._____

WORDS: Sts. 1-3, Billema Kwillia; trans. by Margaret D. Miller; st. 4, Gilbert E. Doan; alt.
MUSIC: Billema Kwillia

Words (st. 4) © 1972 Contemporary Worship 4: Hymns for Baptism and Holy Communion. Reprinted by permission of Augsburg Fortress;
trans. (sts. 1-3) and music by permission of Lutheran World Federation

220

One Bread, One Body

Refrain

One bread, one bod-y, one Lord of all, one cup of bless-ing which we bless. _____ And we, though man-y through-out the earth, we are one bod-y in this one Lord. _____

1. Gen-tile or Jew,
2. Man-y the gifts,
3. Grain for the fields,

Fine

1. ser-vant or free, wom-an or man, no more.
2. man-y the works, one in the Lord of all. One
3. scat-tered and grown, gath-ered to one, for all.

WORDS: John B. Foley
MUSIC: John B. Foley

221

Take Our Bread

Refrain

Take our bread, we ask you; take our hearts, we love you. Take our lives, O Fa-ther, we are yours, we are yours.

Fine

WORDS and MUSIC: Joe Wise

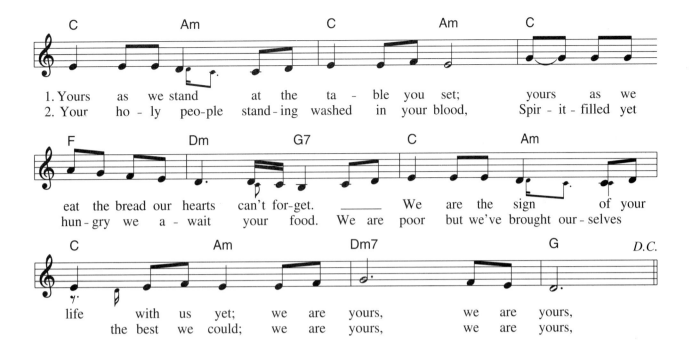

1. Yours as we stand at the ta - ble you set; yours as we
2. Your ho - ly peo-ple stand-ing washed in your blood, Spir - it - filled yet

eat the bread our hearts can't for-get. _____ We are the sign of your
hun - gry we a - wait your food. We are poor but we've brought our - selves

life with us yet; we are yours, we are yours,
the best we could; we are yours, we are yours,

Bread of the World

222

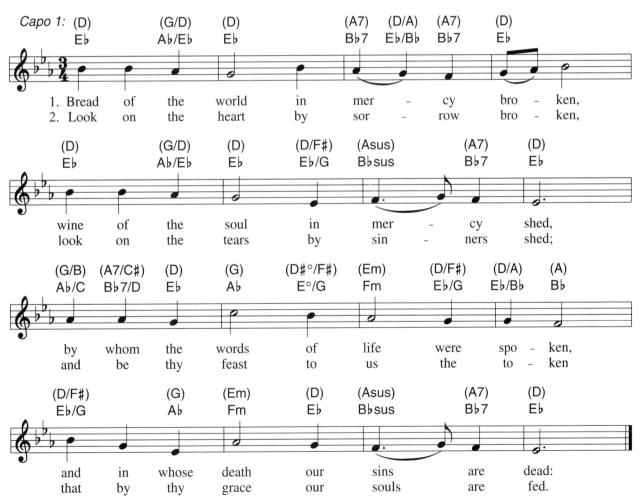

Capo 1:

1. Bread of the world in mer - cy bro - ken,
2. Look on the heart by sor - row bro - ken,

wine of the soul in mer - cy shed,
look on the tears by sin - ners shed;

by whom the words of life were spo - ken,
and be thy feast to us the to - ken

and in whose death our sins are dead:
that by thy grace our souls are fed.

WORDS: Reginald Heber
MUSIC: John S. B. Hodges

223 There Is a Fountain Filled with Blood

Capo 3:

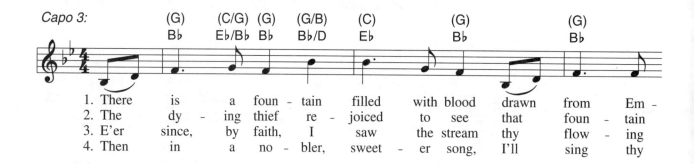

1. There is a foun - tain filled with blood drawn from Em -
2. The dy - ing thief re - joiced to see that foun - tain
3. E'er since, by faith, I saw the stream thy flow - ing
4. Then in a no - bler, sweet - er song, I'll sing thy

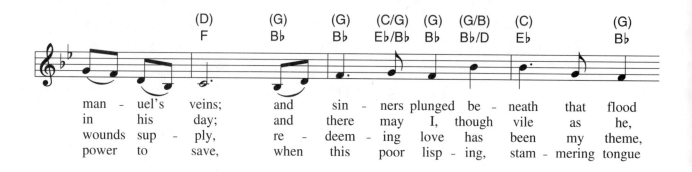

man - uel's veins; and sin - ners plunged be - neath that flood
in his day; and there may I, though vile as he,
wounds sup - ply, re - deem - ing love has been my theme,
power to save, when this poor lisp - ing, stam - mering tongue

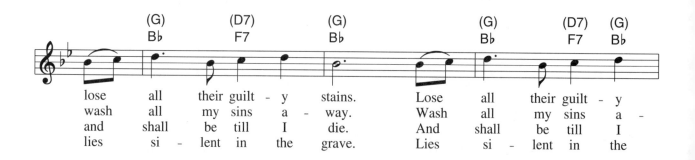

lose all their guilt - y stains. Lose all their guilt - y
wash all my sins a - way. Wash all my sins a -
and shall be till I die. And shall be till I
lies si - lent in the grave. Lies si - lent in the

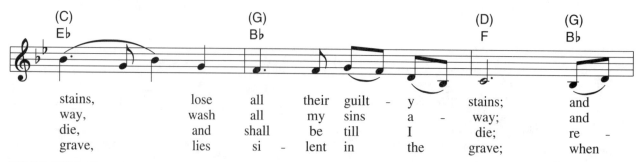

stains, lose all their guilt - y stains; and
way, wash all my sins a - way; and
die, and shall be till I die; re -
grave, lies si - lent in the grave; when

WORDS: William Cowper
MUSIC: 19th cent. USA campmeeting melody

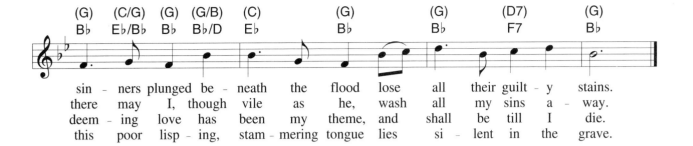

sin - ners plunged be - neath the flood lose all their guilt - y stains.
there may I, though vile as he, wash all my sins a - way.
deem - ing love has been my theme, and shall be till I die.
this poor lisp - ing, stam - mering tongue lies si - lent in the grave.

Come, Be Baptized

224

Come, be bap-tized in the name of the Fa - ther.

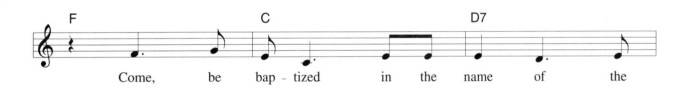

Come, be bap - tized in the name of the

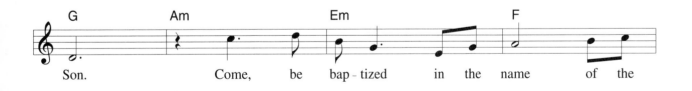

Son. Come, be bap - tized in the name of the

Spir - it. Come, be bap - tized in love.

WORDS and MUSIC: Gary Alan Smith

225

Arise, Shine

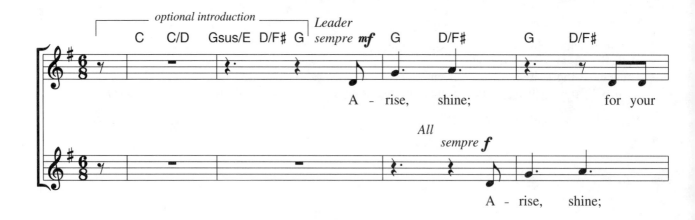

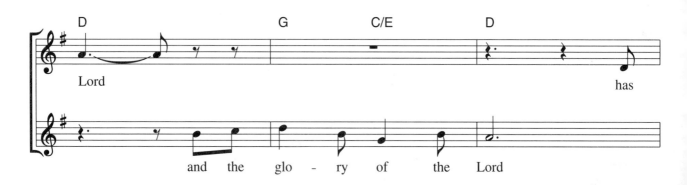

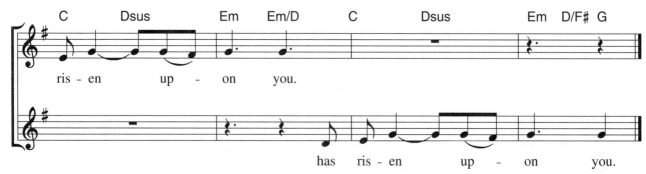

WORDS: Isaiah 60:1
MUSIC: Gary Alan Smith

He Has Made Me Glad
(I Will Enter His Gates)

226

I will en-ter his gates with thanks-giv-ing in my heart, I will

en-ter his courts with praise. I will say, "This is the

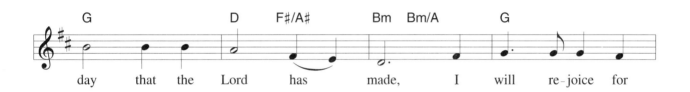

day that the Lord has made, I will re-joice for

he has made me glad." He has made me glad,

he has made me glad, I will re-joice for he has made me

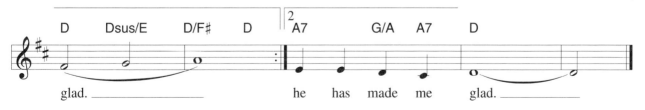

glad. he has made me glad.

WORDS and MUSIC: Leona von Brethorst

227

As We Gather

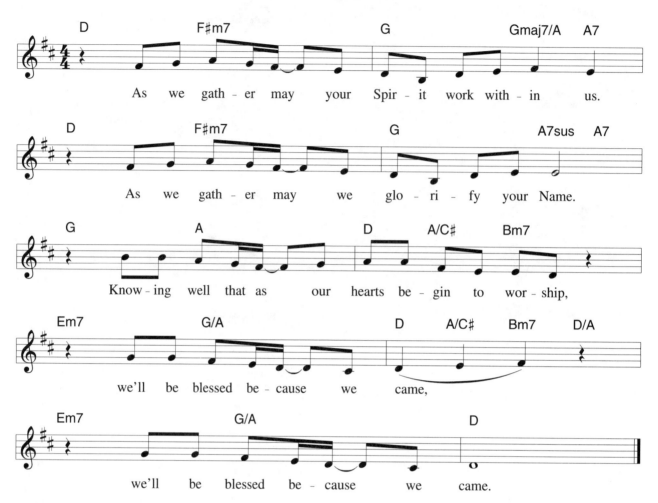

As we gath – er may your Spir – it work with – in us.

As we gath – er may we glo – ri – fy your Name.

Know – ing well that as our hearts be – gin to wor – ship,

we'll be blessed be – cause we came,

we'll be blessed be – cause we came.

WORDS and MUSIC: Mike Fay and Tom Coomes

228

This Is the Day

This is the day, this is the day that the Lord hath made, that the

Lord hath made. Let us re – joice, let us re – joice and be

WORDS: Psalm 118:24; adapt. by Les Garrett
MUSIC: Les Garrett

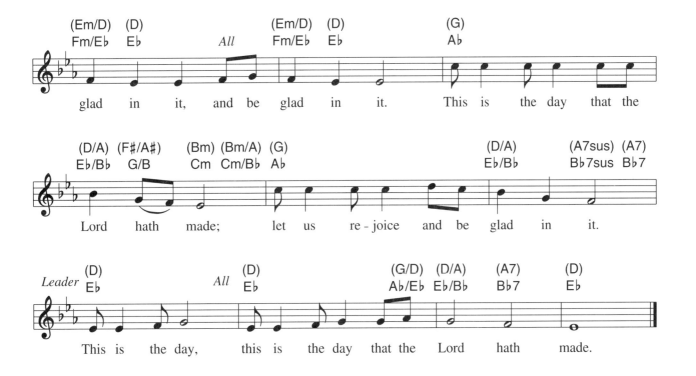

We Bring the Sacrifice of Praise 229

WORDS and MUSIC: Kirk Dearman

230

Sent Forth by God's Blessing

1. Sent forth by God's bless - ing, our true faith con - fess - ing, the peo - ple of God from this dwell - ing take leave. The ser - vice is end - ed, O now be ex - tend - ed the fruits of our wor - ship in all who be - lieve. The seed of the teach - ing, re - cep - tive souls reach - ing, shall blos - som in ac - tion for God and for all. God's grace did in - vite us, and love shall u - nite us to work for God's king - dom and an - swer the call.

2. With praise and thanks - giv - ing to God ev - er liv - ing, the tasks of our ev - ery - day life we will face. Our faith ev - er shar - ing, in love ev - er car - ing, em - brac - ing God's chil - dren of each tribe and race. With your grace you feed us, with your light now lead us; u - nite us as one in this life that we share. Then may all the liv - ing with praise and thanks - giv - ing give hon - or to Christ and that name which we bear.

WORDS: Omer Westendorf
MUSIC: Welsh folk tune

Day Is Dying in the West

1. Day is dy-ing in the west; heaven is touch-ing earth with rest; wait and wor-ship while the night sets the eve-ning lamps a-light through all the sky.

2. Lord of life, be-neath the dome of the u-ni-verse, thy home, gath-er us who seek thy face to the fold of thy em-brace, for thou art nigh.

3. While the deep-ening shad-ows fall, heart of love en-fold-ing all, through the glo-ry and the grace of the stars that veil thy face, our hearts as-cend.

4. When for-ev-er from our sight pass the stars, the day, the night, Lord of an-gels, on our eyes let e-ter-nal morn-ing rise and shad-ows end.

Refrain

Ho-ly, ho-ly, ho-ly, Lord God of Hosts! Heaven and earth are full of thee! Heaven and earth are prais-ing thee, O Lord most high!

WORDS: Mary A. Lathbury
MUSIC: William F. Sherwin

232

May You Run and Not Be Weary

Light pop feel

May you run and not be wea-ry. May your heart be filled with song. _

_ And may the love of God con-tin - ue to give you hope and

keep you strong. And may you run and not be wea - ry. May your

life be filled with joy! _ And may the road you trav - el

al - ways lead you home. _ May you _

WORDS and MUSIC: Paul Murakami and Handt Hanson
© 1991 Changing Church Forum

233

Lord, Dismiss Us with Thy Blessing

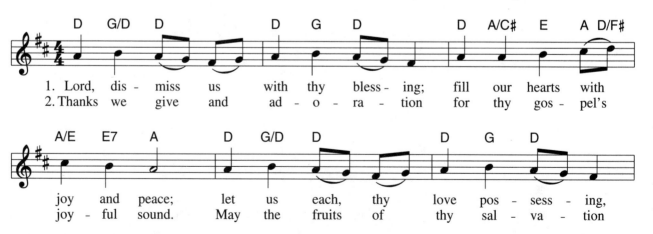

1. Lord, dis - miss us with thy bless - ing; fill our hearts with
2. Thanks we give and ad - o - ra - tion for thy gos - pel's

joy and peace; let us each, thy love pos - sess - ing,
joy - ful sound. May the fruits of thy sal - va - tion

WORDS: Attr. to John Fawcett
MUSIC: *The European Magazine and Review*

tri - umph in re - deem - ing grace. O re - fresh us,
in our hearts and lives a - bound; ev - er faith - ful,

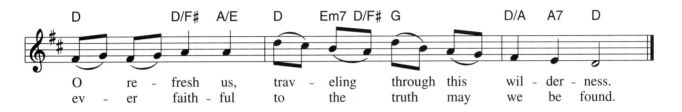

O re - fresh us, trav - eling through this wil - der - ness.
ev - er faith - ful to the truth may we be found.

Let Us Now Depart in Thy Peace 234

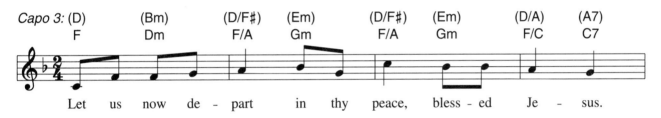

Let us now de - part in thy peace, bless - ed Je - sus.

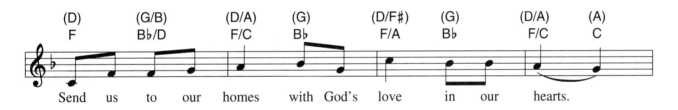

Send us to our homes with God's love in our hearts.

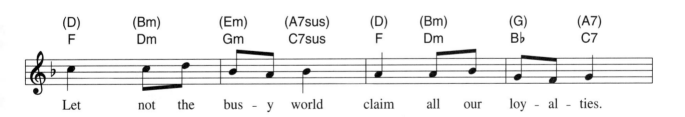

Let not the bus - y world claim all our loy - al - ties.

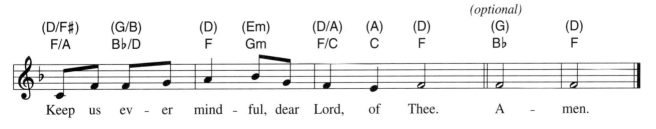

Keep us ev - er mind - ful, dear Lord, of Thee. A - men.

WORDS and MUSIC: New Mexican folk song; adapt. by Lee Hastings Bristol, Jr.

Adapt. © 1961 Concordia Publishing House

235 God Be with You till We Meet Again

1. God be with you till we meet again; by his coun-sels guide, up-
2. God be with you till we meet again; neath his wings se-cure-ly
3. God be with you till we meet again; when life's per-ils thick con-
4. God be with you till we meet again; keep love's ban-ner float-ing

hold you, with his sheep se-cure-ly fold you;
hide you, dai-ly man-na still pro-vide you;
found you, put his arms un-fail-ing round you;
o'er you, smite death's threat-ening wave be-fore you;

God be with you till we meet a-gain. Till we meet, till we

meet, till we meet at Je-sus' feet; till we

meet, till we meet, God be with you till we meet a-gain.

WORDS: Jeremiah E. Rankin
MUSIC: William G. Tomer

236 Shalom

Sha-lom cha-ve-rim, sha-lom cha-ve-rim, Sha-lom, sha-lom.
Fare-well, dear friends, stay safe, dear friends, have peace, have peace.

Le-hit-ra - ot, le-hit-ra - ot, sha-lom, sha-lom.
We'll see you a-gain, we'll see you a-gain, have peace, have peace.

May be sung as a round.
Pronounced: Shah-lohm Kah-vey-reem, Leh-heet-rah-oht

WORDS: Traditional Hebrew blessing; trans. by Roger N. Deschner
MUSIC: Israeli melody

Trans. © 1982 The United Methodist Publishing House

Give Thanks

237

Capo 3:

Give thanks with a grate-ful heart; give thanks to the

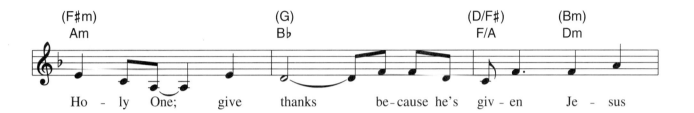

Ho - ly One; give thanks be-cause he's giv-en Je - sus

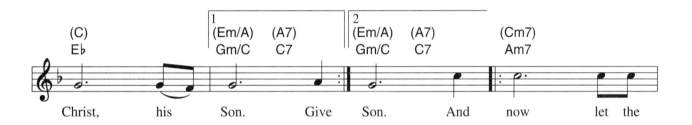

Christ, his Son. Give Son. And now let the

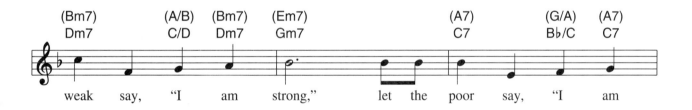

weak say, "I am strong," let the poor say, "I am

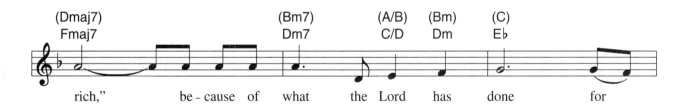

rich," be - cause of what the Lord has done for

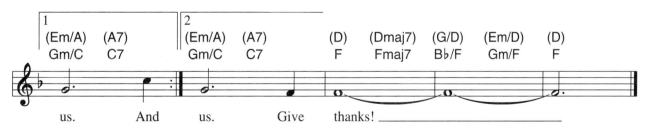

us. And us. Give thanks! _____

238   Come, Ye Thankful People Come

Capo 3:

1. Come, ye thank-ful peo-ple come, raise the song of har-vest home; all is safe-ly gath-ered in, ere the win-ter storms be-gin. God our Mak-er doth pro-vide for our wants to be sup-plied; come to God's own tem-ple, come, raise the song of har-vest home.

2. All the world is God's own field, fruit as praise to God we yield; wheat and tares to-geth-er sown are to joy or sor-row grown; first the blade and then the ear, then the full corn shall ap-pear; Lord of har-vest, grant that we whole-some grain and pure may be.

3. For the Lord our God shall come, and shall take the har-vest home; from the field shall in that day all of-fens-es purge a-way, giv-ing an-gels charge at last in the fire the tares to cast; but the fruit-ful ears to store in the gar-ner ev-er-more.

4. E-ven so, Lord, quick-ly come, bring thy fi-nal har-vest home; gath-er thou thy peo-ple in, free from sor-row, free from sin, there, for-ev-er pu-ri-fied, in thy pres-ence to a-bide; come, with all thine an-gels, come, raise the glo-rious har-vest home.

WORDS: Henry Alford
MUSIC: George J. Elvey

America the Beautiful

WORDS: Katherine Lee Bates
MUSIC: Samuel A. Ward

240

When We All Get to Heaven

1. Sing the won-drous love of Je - sus; sing his mer - cy
2. While we walk the pil - grim path-way, clouds will o - ver -
3. Let us then be true and faith - ful, trust - ing, serv - ing
4. On - ward to the prize be - fore us! Soon his beau - ty

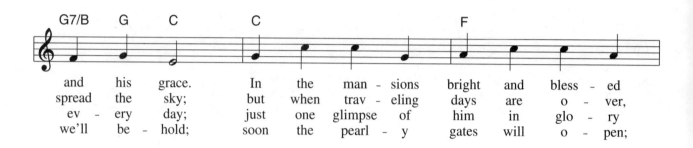

and his grace. In the man - sions bright and bless - ed
spread the sky; but when trav - eling days are o - ver,
ev - ery day; just one glimpse of him in glo - ry
we'll be - hold; soon the pearl - y gates will o - pen;

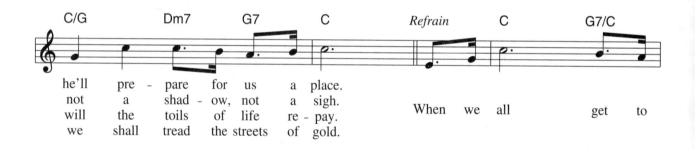

he'll pre - pare for us a place.
not a shad - ow, not a sigh.
will the toils of life re - pay. When we all get to
we shall tread the streets of gold.

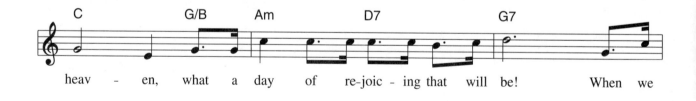

heav - en, what a day of re-joic - ing that will be! When we

all see Je - sus, we'll sing and shout the vic - to - ry!

WORDS: Eliza E. Hewitt
MUSIC: Emily D. Wilson

Hymn of Promise

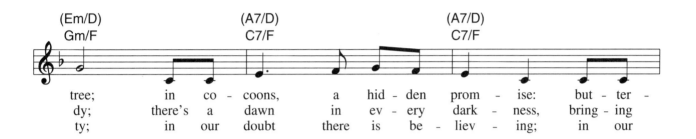

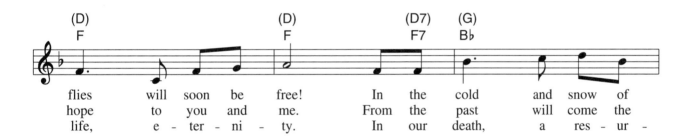

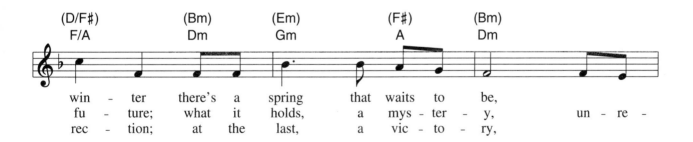

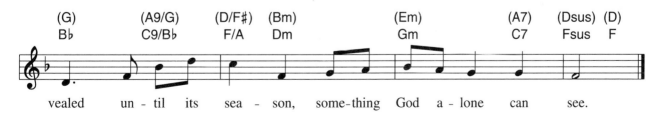

WORDS and MUSIC: Natalie Sleeth

242

Soon and Very Soon

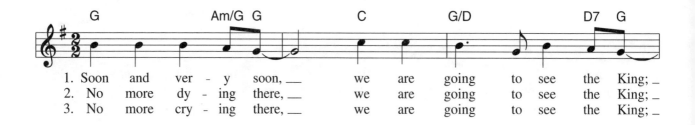

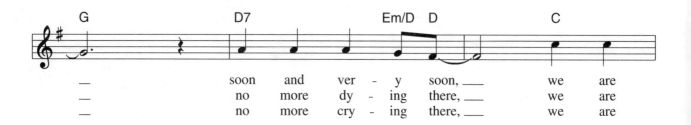

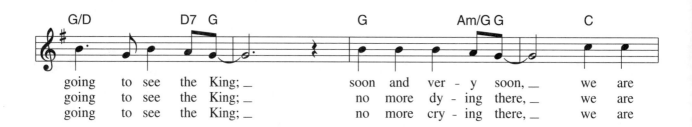

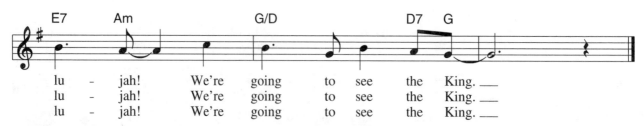

WORDS: Andraé Crouch
MUSIC: Andraé Crouch

Shall We Gather at the River

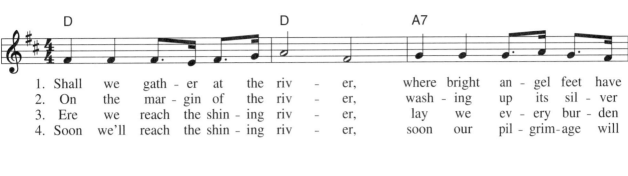

1. Shall we gath-er at the riv - er, where bright an-gel feet have
2. On the mar-gin of the riv - er, wash-ing up its sil-ver
3. Ere we reach the shin-ing riv - er, lay we ev-ery bur-den
4. Soon we'll reach the shin-ing riv - er, soon our pil-grim-age will

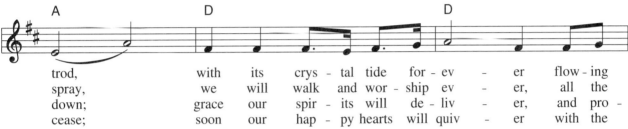

trod, with its crys-tal tide for-ev - er flow-ing
spray, we will walk and wor-ship ev - er, all the
down; grace our spir-its will de-liv - er, and pro-
cease; soon our hap-py hearts will quiv - er with the

Refrain

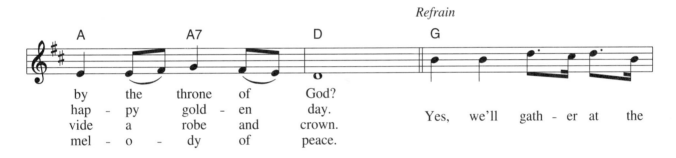

by the throne of God?
hap - py gold - en day.
vide a robe and crown.   Yes, we'll gath-er at the
mel - o - dy of peace.

riv - er, the beau - ti - ful, the beau - ti - ful

riv - er; gath - er with the saints at the

riv - er that flows by the throne of God.

WORDS: Robert Lowry
MUSIC: Robert Lowry

244   # I Sing a Song of the Saints of God

1. I sing a song of the saints of God,
2. They loved their Lord so dear, so dear, and
3. They lived not on - ly in a - ges past; there are

pa - tient and brave and true, who toiled and fought and
his love made them strong; and they fol - lowed the right for
hun - dreds of thou - sands still. The world is bright with the

lived and died for the Lord they loved and knew. And
Je - sus' sake the whole of their good lives long. And
joy - ous saints who love to do Je - sus' will. You can

one was a doc - tor, and one was a queen, and one was a
one was a sol - dier, and one was a priest, and one was
meet them in school, on the street, in the store, in church, by the

shep - herd - ess on the green; they were all of them saints of
slain by a fierce wild beast; and there's not an - y rea - son,
sea, in the house next door; they are saints of God, wheth - er

God and I mean, God help - ing, to be one too.
no, not the least, why I should - n't be one too.
rich or poor, and I mean to be one too.

WORDS: Lesbia Scott
MUSIC: John H. Hopkins, Jr.

I Know Whom I Have Believed

1. I know not why God's won - drous grace to
2. I know not how this sav - ing faith to
3. I know not how the Spir - it moves, con -
4. I know not when my Lord may come, at

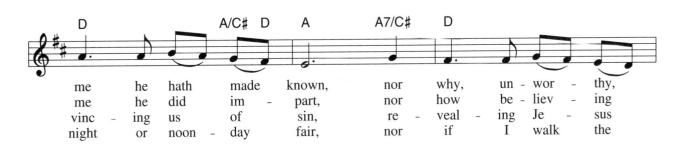

me he hath made known, nor why, un - wor - thy,
me he did im - part, nor how be - liev - ing
vinc - ing us of sin, re - veal - ing Je - sus
night or noon - day fair, nor if I walk the

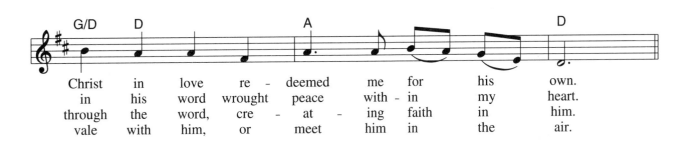

Christ in love re - deemed me for his own.
in his word wrought peace with - in my heart.
through the word, cre - at - ing faith in him.
vale with him, or at meet him in the air.

Refrain

But I know whom I have be - liev - ed, and am per -

suad - ed that he is a - ble to keep that which I've com-

mit - ted un - to him a - gainst that day.

WORDS: Daniel W. Whittle (2 Tim. 1:12)
MUSIC: James McGranahan

246   The Battle Hymn of the Republic

WORDS: Julia Ward Howe
MUSIC: USA campmeeting tune

On Jordan's Stormy Banks I Stand

*Pronounced "Jerdan's"

WORDS: Samuel Stennett
MUSIC: *The Southern Harmony*

248 Marching to Zion

1. Come, we that love the Lord, and let our joys be known; join in a song with sweet ac-cord, join in a song with sweet ac-cord and thus sur-round the throne, and thus sur-round the throne.

2. Let those re-fuse to sing who nev-er knew our God; but chil-dren of the heaven-ly King, but chil-dren of the heaven-ly King may speak their joys a-broad, may speak their joys a-broad.

3. The hill of Zi-on yields a thou-sand sa-cred sweets be-fore we reach the heaven-ly fields, be-fore we reach the heaven-ly fields, or walk the gold-en streets, or walk the gold-en streets.

4. Then let our songs a-bound, and ev-ery tear be dry; we're march-ing through Em-man-uel's ground, we're march-ing through Em-man-uel's ground, to fair-er worlds on high, to fair-er worlds on high.

Refrain

We're march-ing to Zi-on, beau-ti-ful, beau-ti-ful Zi-on; we're march-ing up-ward to Zi-on, the beau-ti-ful cit-y of God.

WORDS: Isaac Watts; refrain by Robert Lowry
MUSIC: Robert Lowry

Guitar Chords

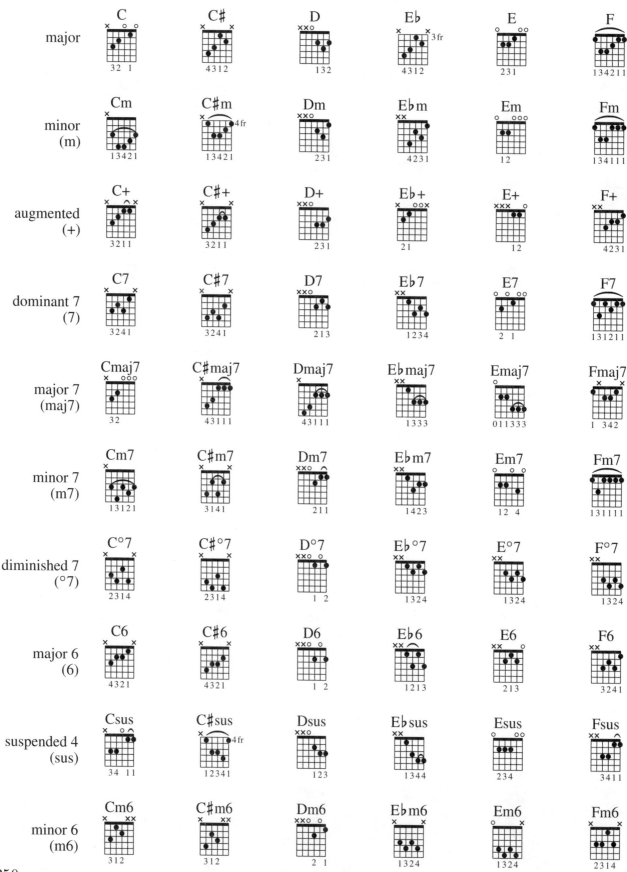

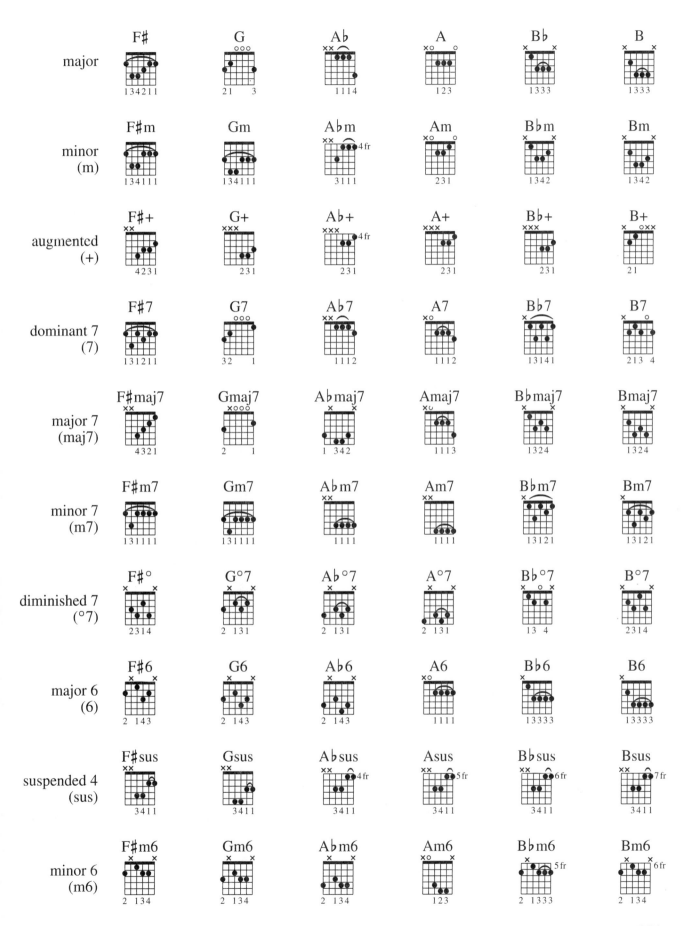

251

INDEX OF COMPOSERS AND AUTHORS

INDEX OF FIRST LINES AND COMMON TITLES